'Jana, I want . . .' Kent muttered brokenly. 'I want to make love to you.'

Stupefied, she gazed up into his face, the lean hardness of his body against hers a physical reflection of the desire in the heavy, dark eyes. A warning bell clanged in her head, clamoured for self-preservation.

'What?' Something inside her snapped. 'You ignore me all evening, can hardly be bothered even to speak to me . . . and then you burst into my room, throw out a . . . friend of mine . . . and then calmly announce you want to make love to me?' Her legs felt as if they were going to give way. 'What do you expect me to do? Throw myself into your arms with cries of gratitude and delight?' Her voice was choking. 'Go to hell, Kent!'

ADORING SLAVE

BY

ROSEMARY GIBSON

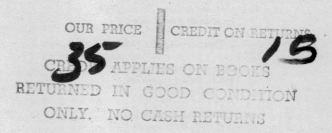

BOOKSTOP
BOOKS

OUR PRICE | CREDIT ON RETURNS
35 **15**
CREDIT APPLIES ON BOOKS
RETURNED IN GOOD CONDITION
ONLY. NO CASH RETURNS

MILLS & BOON LIMITED
ETON HOUSE 18-24 PARADISE ROAD
RICHMOND SURREY TW9 1SR

First published in Great Britain 1989
by Mills & Boon Limited

© Rosemary Gibson 1989

Australian copyright 1989
Philippine copyright 1990
This edition 1990

ISBN 0 263 76454 0

Set in Plantin 11 on 11 pt.
05–9004–49886

Typeset in Great Britain by JCL Graphics, Bristol

Made and Printed in Great Britain

CHAPTER ONE

'AND what the hell happened to you last night?'

'Good morning, Kent. Isn't it a heavenly day? Looks as if summer's finally arrived.' Jana Morton's cheerful greeting was at odds with the wary expression in her wide green eyes as they rested on the lean figure standing with his back to her by the window, gazing out across London.

Her high-heeled court shoes made no sound on the thick russet carpet as she moved quickly over to her desk and sat down. She had anticipated being summoned by the chairman of the Tyson-Moore Advertising Agency shortly after her arrival at work that morning, but she hadn't been prepared to find him actually waiting in her office. He could at least look at her, she thought with sudden resentment as she eyed the broad back.

'I'm waiting for an explanation, not a damn weather report, so cut out the Pollyanna routine, Jana!' he growled, swinging round abruptly, and, as Jana encountered the impatient blue eyes, eyebrows as dark as his hair drawn in a grim line across his forehead, she rather wished that he had kept his back to her.

'You were supposed to be acting as my hostess—and the moment my back was turned you vanished like some bloody rabbit down a hole!'

'I left a message for you at reception,' Jana reminded him stiffly, irritated by the simile, the implication being that she had retreated from an awkward situation like a gauche, nervous teenager in a panic. She considered that her abrupt departure from the Mayfair restaurant the previous evening had been wholly justified, and certainly more diplomatic than the alternative course of action.

'Saying you had a headache?' His firm mouth twisted caustically as he crossed the room with swift, fluid strides and came to an abrupt halt in front of the desk, arms folded imperiously across his powerful chest.

Jana tilted her head upwards, meeting the icy gaze squarely, determined not to be intimidated by the towering figure.

'Would you have preferred I told the truth? That I was sick to death of being mauled about by Ben Sinclair?' With disdain, she recalled the moment when the Canadian businessman, considerably the worse for wear having imbibed a great quantity of wine with the excellent dinner, had moved his hand caressingly up her left leg and, without any attempt at subtlety, suggested that she share his bed for the night. It had taken every ounce of self-control to curb her instinctive response. Wryly, Jana imagined how Kent would have reacted if she had given in to temptation and slapped the man with whom the agency had recently signed a large, profitable account resoundingly around the face.

'Damn it all, Jana, you were only on your own with Ben for five minutes!' Kent raked a lean hand through his thick, dark hair in the by now familiar gesture of exasperation.

'Why should I put up with being pawed about for even five minutes?' Jana demanded heatedly, eyes the colour of dark jade glinting with indignation and incredulity. Surely Kent couldn't seriously be implying that she should have just sat there, smiling sweetly . . . 'Hell, you don't . . .'

'Cut that out!' he intervened forcefully, his eyes narrowing to bright blue slits.

Illogically, his order restored her sense of humour, Kent being the last person to reprove her for the oath, considering his own choice epithets whenever things didn't go exactly as he planned. And last night, Jana admitted ruefully, had most definitely not gone according to plan.

What had been intended as a business dinner between Kent and Ben Sinclair, managing director of the Canadian chain store that was shortly due to launch the exclusive range of 'Freedom' casual wear and cosmetics on to the market, had rapidly turned into a social occasion. Jana's role had been to entertain the Canadian's beautiful nineteen-year-old daughter, leaving the two men free to discuss the impending campaign. But the Canadian girl, her interest in Kent made obvious the moment he was introduced, had spent the entire evening trying to monopolise his attention, quite blatantly inviting him to dance at one point—the point at which Jana had been left to fend off Ben's intoxicated, amorous advances.

Jana had been secretly embarrassed for the younger girl, sensing Kent's irritation, though with a tact she had not hitherto suspected in a man more used to speaking his mind bluntly he had concealed it beneath a mask of cool, tolerant politeness. Part of Jana had also understood the other girl's attraction to the dark man. He was by no means a handsome man in the strictest sense, but the harsh, flagrantly male features, the muscular physique that seemed to be emphasised rather than concealed by expensive tailoring, coupled with the unmistakable aura of wealth and power, were a potent combination.

'Did you take a taxi home last night?' he suddenly demanded brusquely.

'Of course I did!' Jana tried, a little unsuccessfully, not to snap back her retort. Surely he credited her with more sense than to roam around the London streets on her own late at night.

'Straight home?'

Jana scowled down at her desk. 'No, I stopped off for a quick moonlight dip in the Serpentine first,' she muttered caustically, 'and then . . .'

'I called your flat,' he broke in curtly, evidently not appreciative of her humour.

Her eyes clouded with irritation, knowing that he hadn't telephoned merely to express his disapproval at her defection—that surely could have waited until the morning? No, it was far more likely that he had been checking up on her, evidently thinking her incapable of making her own way home in safety.

'Where were you?' he barked.

'That's . . .' She bit her tongue to stop the instinctive response to tell Kent that it was none of his damn business where she was or what she did outside office hours. Her job was tenuous enough as it was; antagonising Kent would hardly make that position any more secure.

'I stayed with a friend,' she said reluctantly. She certainly wasn't going to admit that, as she'd scrambled into the taxi the night before, she had somehow managed to spill the entire contents of her handbag on to the pavement. She had thought she'd gathered up all her strewn possessions, but on arriving back at her flat had discovered that her door keys were missing. Fortunately she kept a spare set at work, but rather than go charging back into central

London at that time of night she had gratefully accepted the offer of a bed made up by the girl in the adjacent flat.

Jana raised her eyes to the craggy face, wondering if Kent's sudden silence indicated that he was waiting for her to offer some form of apology—and that, she decided stubbornly, she was not prepared to do. If anyone should apologise, it ought to be Ben. She tried to gauge what was going on behind the shuttered expression, and as usual failed dismally.

'It wasn't exactly a successful evening, was it?' she tried tentatively.

'A total waste of time might be a more accurate description,' he said tersely, and, evidently deciding that he had already wasted more than enough time on his secretary, he moved purposefully towards the inner office.

Jana watched his retreating figure with a mixture of relief and perplexity. When Kent had pounced on her the moment she'd set foot inside the door that morning, she had mentally steeled herself for battle—and it had all fizzled out to nothing. A small, mocking smile tugged at the corners of her wide mouth. After working with him for the past four months, she should know that there was never anything predictable about Kent Tyson.

She stretched out a hand to retrieve the stack of papers in her pending tray, wondering if the day would ever come when she managed to clear even half of it, and turned her head, concealing a sigh, as the outer door opened.

'Morning,' the messenger grinned cheerily as he placed a large pile of mail on her desk.

'Thanks!' She smiled back wryly.

'Keep you out of mischief,' he returned with a

cheeky grin, and disappeared down the corridor, whistling happily. He always commenced his round on the directors' floor and then worked his way down through the tower block with a familiarity that Jana had envied when she first started. She clearly recalled Kent's wrath when on her very first day it had taken her nearly twenty minutes to discover the whereabouts of the graphics department. She had soon realised that her new employer tolerated no excuses, not even ignorance. If she didn't know something, someone or some place, she was expected to find out—fast.

She started to sort out the mail, dividing it into two categories, those which she could deal with herself or which could be redirected to another department, and those which required some comment from Kent.

She jerked her head up as the intercom buzzed, grabbed for her notebook, and frowned with concentration as Kent, without any preamble, barked out a succession of rapid orders. As usual he seemed to give her a hundred and one tasks to do, and about the same number of seconds in which to complete them. Only once had Jana ever complained about her heavy workload. Kent's answer had been curt and to the point. 'If you can't cope, you know the answer.' She had made certain from that day that she had 'coped'.

'And get me Bob on the line,' he completed his demands, 'and bring through the Thornton file straight away, please.'

'Yes, Kent,' Jana answered swiftly, one hand already grasping the internal telephone.

'And stop frowning. It makes you look like a demented hedgehog.'

'You certainly know how to turn a girl's head,' she

muttered caustically as the intercom crackled into silence, and then grinned as she heard the startled tone of the chief copywriter on the telephone line. 'Sorry,' she murmured swiftly, 'Kent would like a word. I'll put you through.' How had Kent known she was frowning, she wondered absently as she made the connection, her left hand reaching up unconsciously to touch her head.

Two Saturdays ago she had visited a hair salon and rashly ordered her shoulder-length hair to be chopped off. She'd been delighted with the smooth, sculptured bob—at first. As soon as she had washed her hair, it had developed a will of its own and, despite all her efforts to govern it, now stood up around her head in a soft spiky halo—a fact that Kent seemed to take perverse delight in reminding her of. She grimaced, totally unaware of how much the short, gamine style in fact suited her, emphasising the clear, creamy skin, the fragile bone construction, the large, luminous green eyes, shielded beneath thick, sooty lashes.

Briskly, Jana stood up and walked over to the huge cabinet that dominated the far wall, and methodically began to flick her way through the files. She wasn't sure whether she objected more to being likened to a rabbit or a hedgehog. Timid or prickly? Neither analogy was exactly flattering. A smile hovered on her lips as with great clarity she recalled the wife of a client whispering to her dreamily during a business lunch in the directors' dining-room, 'It must be wonderful to work for such a charming man.'

That Kent possessed charm, Jana didn't doubt—but he certainly didn't believe in exercising it on his secretary! Temporary secretary, Jana reminded herself forlornly. Only another few weeks and Kent's permanent personal assistant, a paragon of all the virtues that Jana apparently lacked herself, would be back from her lengthy sick-leave.

She selected a thick grey folder and a little reluctantly walked over to the connecting door, opening it as she heard Kent's response to her light knock.

He was on the telephone, sitting in the padded chair behind the highly polished oak desk, his head bent over a sheet of figures. But any hope Jana had that she might quietly place the folder on his desk and beat a hasty retreat was thwarted when he raised his eyes, frowned, and indicated with a wave of his left hand that she should wait until he had completed his call.

She sat down in the hard-backed chair in front of the desk, her habitual place when taking shorthand, and, rather than look at Kent's chilling expression, she averted her face, letting her eyes travel around the large, imposing room.

A deep leather sofa and two matching armchairs occupied the far end, placed strategically near the drinks cabinet. To the left was an unobtrusive door that led to the small bedroom with en suite bathroom that Kent used when he worked late, which, Jana was aware, was frequently. Once she had come to work early and discovered him at his desk, the tousled dark hair and blue shadow around his square chin making her suspect that he hadn't slept at all. Kent, she mused, looking above his head and through the huge window with its panoramic view over the city, might be a hard taskmaster—but he appeared to be even harder on himself.

She heard the click of the telephone being replaced and reluctantly turned her attention back to him. He had removed the jacket of his lightweight grey suit and the cuffs of his brilliant white shirt were folded back on the tanned, muscular forearms.

For a long minute he scrutinised Jana in silence and for once she could guess exactly what was going through his head—and it wasn't reassuring.

'What exactly possessed you to come to work today dressed like some joker in a holiday camp?' he finally asked conversationally, leaning back in his chair and folding his hands behind his head, the powerful shoulders clearly outlined against the tautening shirt.

Jana wasn't foolish enough to be lulled into a false sense of security by the apparent calmness in his voice, or the deceptive indolence of his posture, but even so she still jumped as he rose abruptly to his feet and glowered down at her.

'For pity's sake, Jana, you're supposed to be my secretary and you come to work dressed like that!'

She flinched as she met the icy blue eyes, knowing that she had been crazy even to hope that Kent might not notice the scarlet, sequined jumpsuit, that she could have remained concealed behind her desk all day.

'I'm sorry,' she tried to keep her voice calm. 'I know this isn't exactly practical for work, but I told you I stayed at a friend's last night. Well, I was a bit pushed for time this morning so I borrowed some of her clothes.'

'And your "friend" normally wears that to work?' His eyebrows rose in disdainful disbelief.

'No, of course not,' Jana said rapidly. 'She's an air hostess and wears a uniform. She hasn't any what you'd call "working" clothes.' The jumpsuit had been the most decorous of all the garments on offer. Jana could just visualise the expression on Kent's face if she'd turned up in the minute denim mini-skirt or the cream, virtually transparent dress with the slit up to the thigh. At least she was decently, if colourfully, covered.

She felt a surge of resentment as Kent continued to survey her as if she were something a more discerning feline wouldn't bother to drag in. It wasn't as if she was in the habit of coming to work dressed like this; normally she wore a smart, businesslike tailored suit.

'If I were a man, you wouldn't be criticising me like this,' she muttered rebelliously.

Kent looked heavenwards, but at least the look of impatience had replaced the one of anger. 'Come on, Jana, you can do better than that!' His eyes narrowed. 'You know damn well I would have reacted exactly the same if a male member of my staff had arrived at work dressed in a clown's suit!'

Jana lowered her eyes, crimson staining her cheeks, not able to remember when she had last felt so humiliated.

'If that's all, Kent, I'll get back to work,' she muttered, her voice seething with resentment. She turned towards the door, raising her chin, trying to salvage some remnants of pride.

'I should say your friend is at least six inches taller than you and of a somewhat different build,' she heard Kent observe to her retreating back.

She didn't deign to reply, ignoring the quick flame of hurt at his implied criticism of her slight figure, that did not fill out the jumpsuit in any of the required places.

'Coffee, please,' were his parting words as she closed the door. She leant against it for a second and took a deep, controlling breath, fighting the almost overwhelming temptation to storm back in and tell him to get his own bloody coffee.

She mustn't let Kent get under her skin, she told

herself forcefully as she walked along the plush carpeted corridor towards the tiny kitchenette situated next to the much larger kitchen that served the directors' dining-room. She mustn't let him provoke her into saying or doing anything that might jeopardise the reference she would need so badly when she left.

She pushed open the door of the kitchenette, almost colliding with the occupant, a tall, fair girl in her mid thirties, Kent's partner's highly efficient PA.

'Sorry, Julie,' she murmured quickly, and then, seeing the older girl's startled look, pleaded, 'Don't say a word!' She ran a hand unconsciously over her slim hips. 'Kent's already bawled me out for my "clown's suit".'

'One of those days?' Julie murmured sympathetically.

'It's every day!' Jana grimaced and heaved a deep sigh.

'Well, there's one thing: no one could accuse Kent of nepotism!'

Jana smiled wryly, doubting that Kent would very much care if anyone did. He wasn't influenced by other people's opinions. She filled up the electric kettle and plugged it in at the mains. She seldom bothered to use the percolator unless Kent had clients; he never seemed to notice what he drank as long as it was strong, black and unsweetened. Then with sudden curiosity she glanced at the fair girl who was setting out cups and saucers on a tray.

'Is that what you thought when I first started here? That Kent had only employed me because I was his stepsister?' Julie was one of the few people who knew about her relationship with Kent, not because Jana kept the fact deliberately concealed, but because she

hardly ever thought of him in that light. Stepbrother
seemed to imply a familiarity, a bond, a closeness that
was definitely lacking in their relationship.

'Hardly!' the other girl answered immediately. 'I
know Kent better than that. He wouldn't have given
you the job if he hadn't thought you capable of doing
it.' She shrugged. 'You just happened to be in the
right place at the right time. He was pretty desperate
when Mrs Thomas broke her leg, and didn't have
time to go through all the rigmarole of interviews and
checking references. You were the obvious choice,
living in London and being in between jobs.'

Jana spooned coffee into the cups. 'In between jobs'
was one way of putting it, she supposed; desperate
would have been nearer the truth. Desperate enough
to call Kent and ask if he had any vacancies within his
company. The offer of a temporary post as his
secretary had been not only a surprise, but a godsend.

'Any idea when Mrs T. is due back?' Julie asked
idly as they stood waiting for the kettle to boil.

'A couple of weeks,' Jana answered, trying not to
sound too dispirited. She suddenly grinned. 'I'm
surprised she's got a job to come back to, that Kent
didn't sack her on the spot for daring to fall down the
stairs and break a leg during office hours!' She knew
she was being unfair; she herself had placed the
regular order for flowers to be delivered to the middle-
aged widow. She knew, too, that Kent had visited the
hospital on a number of occasions.

'Hey, you really have got it in for Kent today!' Julie
observed, arching her fair eyebrows. 'Have you
always hit it off so well with him? Or is it only
recently you've started to find him so irresistible?'

Jana couldn't help laughing at the other girl's
sarcasm. 'I hardly knew him before I came to

London,' she admitted, and was caught completely off guard by the sudden, sharp sense of loss, the knowledge that she was no nearer knowing Kent now than she had been on that day, four years ago, when he'd first entered her life.

She had been sixteen and still at boarding school when she had received a letter from her actress mother, stating that she had met the most wonderful man in the world, someone she had worked for, years ago, back in Canada. Jana shrugged. Nothing unusual in that. Her mother had a succession of 'wonderful' men; good-looking, aspiring young actors who were clearly besotted with their beautiful, red-headed leading lady. Equally apparent, and embarrassingly so to the young Jana, was that these ardent swains were all some ten years her mother's junior. Jana read on. This particular wonderful man had been widowed three years ago. So? He and her mother had been married two days ago.

Incredulity that her mother had finally settled for any one man had swiftly changed to hurt. Her mother could have at least invited her to the wedding, introduced her to the man who was now her stepfather. Jana cringed. Please, she prayed, don't let him be some young Adonis only a few years older than me.

A week later, Jana had been pulled out of a French lesson and coolly informed that her mother was here to see her. It was an unwritten rule that parents did not come waltzing into the school to visit their offspring at any time they chose, a rule Jana's mother had steadfastly chosen to ignore over the years.

Furious and hurt, Jana had stomped along to the common-room, plotting her revenge. She had flung open the door.

'Mummy, darling! Oh, how I've missed you,' she'd trebled plaintively, dancing into the room and flinging her arms around her dazed-looking parent.

She had turned her attention to the tall figure by her mother's side. Well, at least he looked pretty old, at least thirty and not that much younger than her mother. Neither did he look quite as wet as some of the men she had seen her mother with in the past. Jana had pirouetted in front of him and executed a dainty curtsy.

'And you must be my new daddy,' she had cooed. 'What fun we're all going to have.' She had clasped her hands in front of her and given a little simper. 'I've wanted my very own daddy for such a long time,' she'd warbled, chin trembling, gazing up into the rugged face with wide, innocent eyes.

'And I've always wanted a cute little stepsister,' the man had drawled, before starting to choke. Only then had Jana noticed the third occupant of the room, a tall, grey-haired man, standing by the window.

Of course it should have all been excruciatingly embarrassing, but Jana had been too suffocated with laughter to care. Somewhere, too, had lurked an illogical relief that her mother wasn't married to the man called Kent, but to his father.

'Hey, Jana. The kettle's boiling!' Julie's voice brought her back to earth quickly. 'You were miles away.'

'In another life,' Jana admitted with a tiny smile, and, switching off the kettle, began to pour boiling water into the cups.

The rumblings of Jana's stomach grew louder. Surely Kent would hear them, she thought despairingly, and realise the lateness of the hour? She was sitting in his office, her pencil skimming over the pages of her notepad as she took down his rapid dictation. Kent never paused or backtracked; he spoke concisely and quickly, and Jana, not for the first time, was intensely grateful for her proficient shorthand.

'Yours, etc. . . .'

She breathed a sigh of relief, slammed her notebook shut, and flexed her aching fingers. Kent was sitting behind his desk, the late evening rays of sun touching his head, igniting small, blue flames in the thick, dark hair.

'Do you want this transcribed immediately?' she asked, unable to keep the weariness from her voice.

'It can wait until Monday.'

'Right.' She rose to her feet. 'Goodnight then, Kent.' She started towards the door.

'Is your passport up to date?'

'What?' She spun round and surveyed him with large, startled eyes. 'I haven't actually got one,' she admitted, frowning her bewilderment at the abruptness of the question. 'I was only a baby when we came back from Canada so I was still on my mother's, and when I went to France last year I used a visitor's passport . . .'

'OK, OK, I get the picture.' Kent groaned, raising his hands in front of him as if to ward off a physical attack.

'Don't worry, I'm not about to produce my holiday snaps!' she said cuttingly.

He ignored her remark. 'Just get a passport. Pronto.'

Jana stood motionless waiting for him to continue, but he bent his head over the open file on his desk, apparently now completely oblivious of her presence.

She felt like placing a hand on each side of the broad,
powerful shoulders and shaking him until his teeth
rattled. Except her efforts would probably be as
ineffectual as a summer breeze attempting to fell an
oak tree.

'Am I permitted to know why I should need a
passport "pronto"?' she demanded icily, unable to
remain silent any longer.

He glanced up. 'Oh, didn't I tell you?' he
murmured with an innocence that set her teeth on
edge. 'When I go to Calgary at the end of the month
to launch the Freedom campaign, I'm taking you with
me.'

For a moment, she was only aware of a rush of
delight, soft colour staining her cheeks with
excitement, and then came the familiar burst of
irritation. He hadn't asked her to go, hadn't even
ordered her to go; he had just calmly announced it as a
fait accompli, taking it for granted that she was bound
to fall in with his wishes. She didn't feel like shaking
him; she could hit him! Then common sense flooded
to the fore. She wanted desperately to go to Canada,
had never even in her wildest dreams imagined that
Kent would be taking her on this business trip. No, it
would be stupid to say anything that might make him
change his mind; decidedly undiplomatic to remind
him huffily that strictly speaking at the end of the
month she would no longer be in his employ.

She raised her head and was disconcerted to see the
blue gleam in the brilliant eyes, realising then that he
had been fully aware of the battle going on inside
her—and had been amused by it.

'I'll make all the necessary travel arrangements,' she
said coolly. 'On Monday,' she added rapidly. If she
started now, she would be here all night.

Kent leaned back in his chair. 'Book the outward flight for the twenty-sixth.'

Jana frowned. 'But that's five days early,' she said hesitantly. The campaign had been planned to coincide with the Calgary Stampede, beginning on the first Friday in July.

'I'm taking a few days' break,' he told her, adding laconically, 'going to look up some friends. Maybe fit in a camping-trip.'

'Oh, I see.' Her forehead creased uncertainly. 'Shall I book my flight for the Thursday, then? Or what?'

'You insist on separate planes?' His mouth quirked as he surveyed her, his eyes half closed beneath the dark lashes.

'It's my boarding-school upbringing!' she retorted tartly. 'So what do I do while you're out communing with the Great Outdoors?'

'You object to a few days' holiday?' he drawled back. 'A chance to see something of Canada?'

'What?' she wondered if she had heard him correctly. 'Are you teasing me?' she demanded suspiciously. She studied his face and was taken aback by the serious intensity in his eyes.

'Sit down, Jana,' he ordered her quietly. 'There's something you should know.'

Without warning, her whole body stiffened, cold fingers reached out and clutched her heart. There was a hesitancy in the normally decisive voice, a hesitancy she had only ever heard once before.

Weakly, she perched on the edge of the chair, knuckles white as they lay in her lap, staring at Kent but not seeing him, remembering only that other time . . . Her last term at secretarial college in Bournemouth. Being summoned to the Principal's office. Apprehension changing to surprise and pleasure at seeing Kent's tall figure dominating the small room. Then only numbness as he took hold of her hands and gently told her that her mother and stepfather were both dead. Drowned in a freak boating accident off the Dorset coast. She closed her eyes . . .

'Jana, are you all right?' Her eyes flew open. Kent was standing over her, his eyes dark with concern.

'Yes, I'm fine,' she muttered, the panic ebbing as she pushed those nightmare images firmly back into her subconscious. 'Really,' she added quickly, seeing the look of disbelief on his face. 'What were you going to tell me?' She frowned up at him.

'It'll keep,' he said quietly, moving back to his desk. 'Go on home now, Jana.'

'But . . .' She closed her mouth, knowing it was useless to protest. If Kent said it would keep, nothing she could say would dissuade him. Resignedly she rose to her feet.

She spent a few minutes tidying up her desk, giving her pending tray one last baleful glare. Still, it wouldn't be her problem for much longer, she reminded herself as she picked up her cream jacket and handbag and headed down the corridor. A wave of depression suddenly engulfed her. Kent had given her a short reprieve, but it didn't solve the long-term problem. She smiled wryly as she entered the lift, knowing that one of the reasons she had delayed applying for other jobs was the unrealistic hope that Kent might suddenly decide she was indispensable and offer her a permanent position on his staff. Working for Kent might be exhausting but it was also fascinating, and it wasn't going to be easy finding anything anywhere near as interesting. Jana grimaced. It wasn't going to be easy finding another job, full

stop! Her face cleared. Surely, armed with a reference
from a man of Kent's standing in the business world,
the prospects would be less grim than before.
Despondently she thought back to those nerve-
racking interviews, the awful moment when she was
required to give details of her past employment . . .

The lift doors glided open and Jana walked through
the foyer, smiling at the security guard as she stepped
out on to the pavement.

The tube station was practically deserted—one
consolation for the late hours she worked was that she
nearly always missed the rush hour. On the platform
she sat down on the seat and without much
enthusiasm contemplated the bleak weekend ahead.
She hadn't been in London long enough to make any
real friends, and she had had to shelve her plans for
enrolling on a French evening course and joining a
local sports club. The long hours imposed by Kent
made any form of regular social commitment
impossible. She sighed ruefully, remembering how
during her year in digs in Bournemouth she'd longed
for the day when she could come to London, be
independent, and have her own flat. It had come as a
shock to discover that she wasn't quite as self-
sufficient as she would have liked to believe. She had
been forced to admit that she missed the
companionship of her old schoolfriends, the girls with
whom she had shared digs. Solitude in the past had
been a luxury, never a state enforced upon her.
Nothing had quite prepared her for those periods of
aching loneliness.

The tube train drew in, and as Jana stepped on, she
grinned wryly. Snap out of it, she ordered herself. She
was going to Canada. Her mood immediately lifted, a
tingle of excitement coursing through her. She wasn't

only going to Canada, but actually to Calgary, the city where her mother had lived, where she herself had been born. What had Kent been about to tell her? Unbidden, a wave of uneasiness stirred inside her. Kent had known her mother all those years ago in Canada, so therefore . . . No! That was a line of thought she adamantly refused to pursue. It was something she had come to terms with a long time ago. She had her own life to lead now—the past couldn't affect her and should remain buried.

She alighted at the station at Stockwell, and, emerging into the dusk, walked briskly down Clapham Road into Clapham High Street, turning left into a cul de sac. She pushed open the outer door of a converted Victorian house and ran up the first flight of narrow stairs to her flat. She fished out the keys from her handbag, opened the door and froze, staring into the room with stunned, shocked eyes.

CHAPTER TWO

NAUSEA tightened Jana's throat as she surveyed the chaos that had once been her orderly lounge. Books were strewn everywhere, furniture upturned, obscene graffiti daubed in violent red paint on the cream walls.

Well, she had been contemplating redecorating, she thought with mounting hysteria, and grabbed a chair, sitting down quickly before her legs gave way. The police. She must call them straight away—if she could find the telephone . . .

She discovered it discarded on the floor, beneath a cushion, but still intact. The policeman who took her call, after ensuring that she herself was unharmed, warned her that it might be several hours before someone would be sent to see her. Several hours! She registered the words with growing desperation, the need for human company overwhelming her. If only the girl next door wasn't away on a night flight . . . Then it suddenly became imperative that she draw the curtains and switch on every light in the flat, even in the small bathroom.

A scene of destruction greeted her in every room, the bedroom the most appalling. The bed had been upturned against the wall, the mattress slashed, her clothes dragged out from the cupboard and chest of drawers, and shredded to ribbons. Even the framed photograph of her mother had been smashed, broken glass lying in fragments on the floor. Jana started to shake uncontrollably. It was the vindictiveness, the

sheer and utter futility of it all. She had nothing worth
stealing, no expensive stereo, no video, just an old
black and white television set, a hair-dryer, a small
amount of cash kept in the top drawer of her chest.
She always wore her most valuable possession, the
gold wristwatch given to her by her mother on her
eighteenth birthday.

Biting back the tears, Jana walked slowly back into
the lounge and picked up the telephone. There was no
one else to call. He might still be at work, might be on
his way out for the evening . . .

'Oh, Kent!' She could have shouted out her relief as
she heard the deep, familiar voice in her ear. 'My
flat's been broken into . . .' Her voice wouldn't stop
trembling. 'It's . . . so awful . . .'

He didn't waste words, just said decisively 'I'll be
straight over,' and replaced the receiver.

Jana stared down at the telephone, still in her hand.
She had known he would come, known he wouldn't
even hesitate, not because he cared, she reminded
herself wryly, but because he felt responsible for her.
It was a responsibility he had assumed, unasked, since
the day her mother had died.

Jana's eyes darkened. Kent had not moved from her
side during that terrible, endless day. In those long
hours of shared grief, she had found comfort in those
strong arms, solace in the deep, soothing voice. Then,
after the trauma of the funeral, when she had returned
to college, it had been reassuring to know that Kent
was only a telephone call away if she should need him.

When she had moved to London he had formed the
habit of dropping in to see her during the weekend,
sometimes only staying for a few minutes, sometimes
extending an invitation to go sightseeing. At first she
had looked forward to those shared expeditions with

eagerness and pleasure; then, slowly, had come the realisation that Kent wasn't deliberately seeking her company through choice, but was motivated by a sense of duty. With increasing irritability she had started to refuse his invitations, claiming prior engagements, inventing a non-existent, hectic social life. And he must have believed her excuses, because the impromptu visits, the invitations, the telephone calls had stopped, Kent now evidently satisfied that he had fulfilled his obligations, no doubt relieved that he need no longer waste his precious time on her.

The sharp knock on the door made Jana jump and set her heart pounding, and with it came the shocking knowledge that she no longer felt safe in her own home.

'Who is it?' She couldn't keep the apprehension out of her voice, nor could she stop the surge of relief as she heard Kent's unmistakable voice. She flung open the door, more than a little ashamed of that acute longing just to hurl herself into his arms.

'Are you all right?' he demanded, looking down into her ashen face, and then his mouth tightened as he glanced over her head into the room beyond. Wordlessly, he pushed by her, his eyes hardening as they absorbed the graffiti, the muscles along the lean jawline clenching.

'It's not usually quite this untidy,' Jana tried to joke, but the words seem to come out in a strangled rush. 'I'm afraid I can't offer you any coffee, because all the mugs have been s-smashed.' She started to laugh at the absurdity of her words, which implied that this was some sort of social occasion, and the next second she was being propelled across the room by strong, firm hands and pushed into a chair.

'Drink this,' Kent ordered, producing a hip-flask

from the back of his jeans and pouring a measure into the cap.

She nodded obediently, thinking how easy it was just to let Kent take command. The scalding liquid made her gasp as it hit the back of her throat, but it had the desired effect, sending a tingling warmth coursing through her veins. She watched Kent walk over to the front door, stoop down and examine the lock.

He straightened up, frowning. 'Odd, the lock doesn't appear to have been forced at all.'

'No,' she agreed, and decided that it might be prudent to take another quick gulp of brandy before admitting the truth. Then before she could lose her nerve, she confessed about her lost keys, keys which she kept—for safety—in a small brown purse, together with her spare library tickets. Tickets which just happened to have her name and address on.

'Of all the brainless, stupid things to do!' Kent thundered at her, his whole body tense as he glowered across the room.

Jana didn't answer; she felt too drained, too unbelievably weary even to attempt to defend herself. Besides, what would be the point? Worst of all—Kent was absolutely right. But it would have been nice to have had some sympathy, she decided with a rare spurt of self-pity. Anyone would think she was the criminal and not the victim from the way Kent was scowling down at her. For a second she wished she had never contacted him, wished she had coped with the situation on her own. Perhaps she had ruined his plans for the evening and that was contributing to his anger, though judging from the fact that he was dressed so casually, in jeans and a blue, denim shirt, the sleeves of which were rolled back on the lean, muscular forearms, it didn't appear that he had been on his way to a formal function. She knew so little about his personal life, had no idea of how he spent his time away from the office—or with whom. But she doubted that a man as obviously attractive as Kent would ever want for willing partners to share his evenings and weekends if he chose not to be alone.

'You might just as well have left the door wide open and issued invitations. For heaven's sake Jana, hasn't it occurred to you that the burglar could have come in while you were actually here, at night, in bed?' Blue eyes blazed into hers.

Jana shuddered. Of course she had thought of that. If she hadn't stayed at Linda's last night . . . but then, if she hadn't lost her keys in the first place, she wouldn't have had to. She shook herself mentally, trying to collect her rambling thoughts.

'Jana, I'm sorry.' Suddenly Kent held up his hands in a gesture of peace, and his mouth twisted wryly. 'It's just that . . .'

'I'm a damn nuisance,' she cut in drily, trying to ignore the raw flick of hurt.

'Don't start putting words into my mouth,' he said tersely, 'I was only . . .' Whatever he was going to say was left unsaid as a sharp knock on the door announced the arrival of a young police constable.

Then Jana had to go through the whole rigmarole of her lost keys again, and she could tell from the expression on the young man's face that his sentiments coincided exactly with Kent's—although he didn't express them quite so forcefully.

'Don't you ever do anything stupid?' she felt like demanding of both men, and suddenly decided that she didn't care much for the male sex. Arrogant chauvinists, the lot of them. Her eyes rested for a moment on the dark head.

As soon as they were alone, Kent turned to her abruptly. 'Is there someone you can stay with tonight?'

She frowned, that particular problem having not yet occurred to her. Somehow all her thoughts had been focused on this room and the present. One thing was for certain—she didn't want to stay in her flat tonight. An icy shiver crept up her spine at the thought that somewhere out there in the darkness lurked a stranger with access to her home.

'No,' she answered finally. 'The girl next door's away.'

'You'll have to stay at my flat then.'

Jana stiffened at the reluctance in his voice. Pride demanded that she refuse the invitation but she had no real alternative than to accept, but she didn't seem to have the energy for even a token protest. 'Thanks,' she muttered ungraciously.

'Come on, then,' he commanded abruptly, and she didn't need any further persuasion, suddenly desperate to get out of the flat. As she slammed the door behind her she felt as if she never wanted to see it again.

Jana stared out through the windscreen into the darkness, conscious of the silent man by her side. Not that Kent ever did indulge in idle conversation, she reminded herself. She turned her head slightly, flicking a glance at the harsh, craggy profile illuminated by the street lights. Strong, lean, capable hands rested lightly on the steering-wheel directing the powerful car towards Kensington.

Was he still angry with her, resenting having her foisted on him for the night? She sighed and her thoughts raced back to her flat and the arduous task that lay ahead in the morning of trying to create some sort of order out of the chaos. She supposed that she would be able to replace most of her broken belongings in time. Except for her clothes—they would have to be replaced immediately.

'Kent.' She murmured his name hesitantly and frowned. He had given no indication that he was even aware of her presence in the car. 'Kent,' she repeated more forcefully, and added in a quick rush, 'May I please have a sub on this month's salary?'

'What?' His dark eyebrows knitted across his forehead. 'Don't I pay you enough?' he demanded curtly.

'Of course you do,' she assured him unhappily. 'It's just that I'm a bit short of funds this week, and I'm going to have to buy a whole new wardrobe—unless I turn naturist.'

'What the hell do you spend your money on?' he asked wearily, making her feel like a child that had run up a slate at the local sweet shop.

'Nightclubs, casinos, horses, men—all the usual, everyday things,' she bit back. Didn't he have an idea of the ordeal she had just been through, any comprehension of the way she was feeling—without putting her through this mindless question-and-answer routine? She must have been mad to imagine even for a second that Kent would be capable of sympathy. Then something inside her seemed to snap as she looked at the granite face. 'For pete's sake, I'm only asking for an advance, not shares in the bloody agency!'

She didn't seem able to stop now, her voice growing louder and louder. 'You are the most cold-blooded, inhuman bastard that's ever walked this earth! I don't want to go to your damn flat. Stop the car! I want to get out . . . now . . .' Her voice choked into silence and she sat there, stunned, appalled by her outburst, and as the car did come to a halt she thought frantically that Kent had taken her at her word, that he was going to order her out, abandon her in the middle of London. She stared straight ahead, not daring to look into his face, dreading the icy fury in his eyes.

'Feeling better now?'

For a moment she couldn't move, unable to believe that she had heard that calm, unruffled voice. Warily, she flicked a glance at him and saw that he was studying her with dark, quizzical eyes, his hands folded casually behind his head. Slowly it dawned on her that he had been quite deliberately goading her into losing her temper all evening. And even more surprising was the fact that she did feel better. The burst of anger had somehow dispelled that awful feeling of hopeless lethargy, which she supposed must have been shock. Despite herself, she couldn't help giving Kent a small, reluctant grin. She couldn't pretend that she had enjoyed his method—but it certainly seemed to have proved as effective as any amount of the sympathy she would have preferred. In fact, she had a strong suspicion that if Kent had been more sympathetic, been nicer to her, she would have simply burst into tears.

'I'm sorry, Kent,' she murmured quietly, feeling that she owed him some sort of apology.

He shrugged and started up the engine, and then, before moving back into the stream of traffic, turned to her with the rare, gentle smile that softened the grim, harsh features, made him look younger, more approachable—and made Jana's heart skip an unexpected beat. 'Hungry?' he enquired quietly.

She smiled back, nodding, not quite trusting herself to speak.

Absently, Jana tossed green salad in the wooden bowl, her attention concentrated on the figure standing by the stove tending two steaks on the eye-level grill. When Kent had asked if she was hungry, she had automatically assumed he was inviting her to a restaurant for a meal. She hadn't realised that he had been nominating himself as the chef. And, judging from the competent ease with which he had made the pepper sauce to accompany the fillet steaks, a very able one.

'Nearly ready,' he informed her. 'Could you lay the table? Knives and forks over there.'

She fished out the cutlery from the pine unit he had indicated and walked the length of the immaculate, modern kitchen to the adjoining dining-area.

There was something oddly intimate about being in Kent's flat, helping him prepare their communal meal—although her assistance had been limited to peeling potatoes and washing lettuce—and she was suddenly overwhelmingly grateful that the idiotic, romantic dreams she had woven around Kent as a schoolgirl had long faded.

Unwillingly her eyes were drawn to the broad shoulders, the muscular back that tapered to lean hips and long, powerful legs, and she was forced to admit to the occasional pull of attraction, a pull, she acknowledged wryly, that sometimes without warning became an alarming sharp tug. But in that she was hardly unique; there couldn't be many women who were totally immune to Kent's flagrant maleness.

She was almost caught off guard as he suddenly

glanced over his shoulder at her, and quickly she concentrated on setting out two places on the pine table, unconscious of the tell-tale flush in her cheeks.

'Is everything to madam's satisfaction?' Kent enquired with deceptive concern as she took her first mouthful of the perfectly cooked steak.

'Delicious,' she admitted.

'Not bad for a cold-blooded bastard?' he mocked, raising one dark eyebrow at her.

She looked up from her plate. 'I said I was sorry,' she retorted evenly, but found it more difficult than usual to meet the blue eyes. She was sorry—for voicing those words out loud. But she suddenly realised that she had meant them. She guessed that some women would regard his remoteness, his self-sufficiency, his air of cool detachment from those around him as a challenge, but she herself found it oddly chilling. Kent might have physical needs, but she couldn't ever imagine him needing the emotional warmth or support of another human being. Even now, when he was presumably relaxed and at ease, she could sense that intangible barrier that he drew around himself. He might tease her, make the odd flippant remark, but she knew from past experience that if she dared hazard a direct question that might even loosely be interpreted as personal, the blue shutters would fall over his eyes, and his face would become as deadpan and expressionless as a mask.

'Sorry?' she murmured, realising that she hadn't heard a word he had been saying.

'I was just asking if you'd had any luck on the job front yet,' he said idly.

She put down her fork. 'When have I had a chance

to go job-hunting?' she demanded scathingly. 'Most employers aren't too keen on holding interviews at ten o'clock at night!' She swallowed another mouthful and then asked with carefully assumed nonchalance, 'I suppose you wouldn't consider keeping . . .'

'No.'

For a moment she was speechless, dumbfounded by the quiet but emphatic refusal. He hadn't even let her finish her sentence, hadn't considered her request for even a second.

'Come on, Kent, don't beat about the bush. Just give me a straight answer,' she muttered savagely under her breath, cutting ferociously into her steak.

If he heard her, he gave no indication, merely gave her a long, thoughtful look, before saying quietly. 'Thornton's are looking for secretaries at the moment. I could have a word with David.'

'No, thanks,' she retorted stiffly. She wasn't good enough for him but she would do for a rival company. 'I'm quite capable of getting a job on my own merit.'

'Now you'll have a reference?'

She looked at him in silence, her eyes dark green with suspicion. 'You know, don't you?' she said finally. 'You checked up on me.' She felt an illogical sense of betrayal.

'Yes,' he agreed. 'I was curious to know what had made you desperate enough to ask me for a job.'

So he had known how difficult it had been to ask him, guessed at the number of times she had dialled his number and then put the telephone down.

'What did Carrington's say?' she asked eventually, staring at him across the table.

'They were pretty evasive,' he admitted and then added with a raised eyebrow, 'but implied that you were something of a trouble-maker.'

'Wonderful!' Jana retorted bitterly. 'But you decided to risk it anyway?' she added caustically.

'I was intrigued to know exactly what kind of trouble you were going to cause,' he murmured, with a slow, infuriating grin.

'Sorry I disappointed you!' she snapped, irked by that grin.

He pushed his plate to one side, folded his arms across his chest, and surveyed her with brilliant eyes. 'So what did you do, Jana? Organise a work-to-rule because the coffee-machine broke down?'

The amused tolerance in his voice set her blood boiling, forced the indiscretion, made her forgetful of her vow never to tell him.

'I did what I should have done to Ben Sinclair last night. I slapped the MD in the face!' Then she could have quite easily stretched out a hand and slapped Kent's lean face as he gave a deep chuckle.

'Sexual harassment is not funny!' she said witheringly, fighting down her rising temper. 'And before you say anything else, I did not ask for it. I'm not in the habit of wiggling my hips and fluttering my eyelashes at the boss!' Bitterly she recalled the insinuations made by prospective employers when with naïve honesty she had told the truth about her abrupt departure from Carrington's, the scepticism in the male eyes, the implications that she couldn't possibly be as innocent as she claimed. Of course it hadn't helped matters when Carrington's refused point blank to give her a reference. Jana sighed, and then her innate sense of humour, never far below the surface, came to the fore. 'I can't help it if middle-aged men find me irresistible!' But it hadn't been funny at the time, nor had the ensuing two months' unemployment. Perhaps it also explained why she had felt such a fierce, burning resentment against Ben Sinclair the previous evening.

She smiled wryly at Kent and was disconcerted to find him studying her with dark, serious eyes, all trace of mockery and amusement vanished.

'Why didn't you tell me this before? When it happened?' he demanded quietly.

'Because it was my problem,' she retorted swiftly. 'I didn't need your help.' Then the sheer irony of the words struck her—because in the end she had turned to him for help, in the same way as she had turned to him tonight. And on neither occasion, she realised with growing shame, had she even thanked him properly.

She ate the rest of her meal mechanically, grateful that Kent, too, had lapsed into silence, and as soon as they had both finished she jumped abruptly to her feet.

'I'll wash up, as you cooked,' she volunteered, picking up the empty plates.

'Shall we toss a coin to see who makes the coffee?' he commented drily, following her through into the kitchen.

In the end he helped her with the washing-up, and again Jana was struck by that peculiar sense of intimacy in performing the domestic chore together. Except that it didn't seem to make her feel closer to Kent; on the contrary, she felt an uncomfortable awareness of him as he stood just a few inches away, drying up the knives and forks as she placed them in the rack. Then there was that moment when his fingers accidentally brushed her hand as he placed a plate in her bowl of hot, soapy water, and she had the ridiculous desire to snatch it away. Suddenly, she longed to go to bed, to close her eyes, and shut off the whole world.

They carried their coffee through to the living-room, and Jana sat down on the pristine white sofa, wishing she felt relaxed enough to flick off her shoes and curl her legs up under her.

Tonight was the first time she had ever been inside Kent's flat, and she was forced to admit to a certain amount of disappointment. The living-room was undeniably luxurious, with the thick, plush carpet, the elegant furniture, the subtle grey décor, but it was curiously impersonal. There seemed little of Kent's strong personality impressed on the room—or of anyone else's. Reluctantly, Jana was forced to recognise that unconsciously she had been searching for some indication of feminine influence. Then, as she turned her head, and her eyes alighted on the desk in the alcove, strewn with papers, she couldn't help smiling. Evidently Kent didn't stop working simply because he had left the office.

Her eyes flicked over to him, sprawled out in an armchair, long legs stretched out in front of him. His body was relaxed, his posture indolent, yet his eyes, darkened almost to navy blue in the dim lighting, remained restless, as if he could impose his will on his body, but his mind could never be wholly at ease.

Not for the first time, she wondered what drove him to work twelve hours a day. None of the obvious answers seemed to apply to Kent. Despite his air of command, his unquestionable authority, he was hardly a megalomaniac. Nor was she convinced that it was a desire for material possessions that motivated

him. He didn't surround himself with the normal
trappings associated with a man in his position: no
yacht or executive jet on permanent standby. Even his
flat and car, though undoubtedly expensive, were by
no means ostentatious. She smiled. Perhaps it was
simply the challenge of running a successful business
that attracted Kent—the power and wealth merely a
by-product of that success.

'I gather from your expression that you don't
approve.'

Jana flushed, conscious that she had been staring at
Kent and, judging by the lazy grin on his face, that he
had been perfectly aware of her scrutiny.

'Of the room, I mean,' he added teasingly. 'Colour-
scheme too tame? A splash of lurid orange here and
there?'

'It's very nice,' she retorted evasively, refusing to
bite, knowing that he was mocking her for her passion
for bright colours.

'But?' he prompted.

She shrugged. 'Well, it's not exactly homely, is it?'
It reminded her of something out of a glossy magazine
where no one ever performed mundane everyday
tasks, where no one left dirty mugs on the coffee-table,
or newspapers strewn across the carpet.

'Is that how you see me?' Kent's teeth were very
white against the tan of his skin. 'A pipe and slippers
man? Coming home to the little wife every night? An
adoring spaniel greeting me in the hall?'

'Hardly!' Jana scoffed. 'More like a Roman emperor
surrounded by adoring slaves—of the nubile female
variety,' she added sweetly.

He quirked an eyebrow at her. 'I don't look my best
in a toga. Haven't the legs for it.'

Automatically her eyes were drawn to his jeans,

tautening along the line of his powerful thighs as he casually crossed one leg over a knee. Conscious that her appraisal would not have gone unnoticed by the dark, teasing face, she coloured.

'I wouldn't know,' she said crisply. 'Not being an expert on men's legs.' The look of amusement in his eyes infuriated her. 'And anyway, you don't have to be so scathing! A lot of people would settle for that—a home, a family, somewhere to belong.' Once, she remembered, that was all she had craved from life: a sense of permanency. Her thoughts flickered back over the years, to the school holidays spent wherever her mother happened to be at the time. Holidays in cheap boarding houses, second-rate hotels, shabby bedsits. Of course things had improved once her mother had landed a part in a television soap opera which had turned her into a household name overnight—but even then her mother still had not thought it necessary to provide a permanent home for Jana.

'Is that what you'd settle for?' Kent's voice cut through her thoughts.

'Maybe,' she said cagily, averting her eyes quickly from his too observant scrutiny. Words like security and stability would be anathema to a man like him.

'Jana,' his voice was low and intense, 'I'm not scoffing. It's just not for me. The blissful, domestic bit. Happy families.'

'Too boring, I suppose,' she snapped, and then somewhat spoilt the effect by yawning.

'Come on. Bed. You look wiped out.' He rose to his feet in a swift, controlled movement.

'I am tired,' Jana agreed, scrambling upright, avoiding Kent's helping hand for no logical reason. Then she frowned hesitantly. 'I haven't got a nightie.'

'Sorry, can't help you there.' His eyes gleamed and then he relented. 'Shirt do?' He disappeared into what was presumably his bedroom and appeared a few seconds later, brandishing a cotton shirt.

Jana couldn't stop the grin spreading across her face as she surveyed the bright, lurid checks, finding it impossible to visualise Kent actually wearing it.

'It was a present,' he admitted, tossing it into her arms.

She registered the words in silence, strangely loath to wear something that had presumably been given to Kent by another woman. She doubted that a man would have bought him the shirt as a gift!

'Kent,' she murmured casually, addressing her words to his back as he bent over the sofa and pulled it out to form a bed, 'haven't you anything a little plainer?'

'Thought you wanted something to cover your maidenly modesty, not audition for Dallas in,' he murmured mildly, standing upright, and then a twinge of irritation crossed his face as he saw that she still hadn't moved towards the bathroom. 'OK, I admit it's not exactly Dior, but it's only for one night!' Unexpectedly, he suddenly grinned. 'Actually, I've another half-dozen exactly the same. My aunt sends me one each year for Christmas from Vancouver.'

Jana immediately forgot all about the shirt, her face alight with curiosity. 'I didn't know you had family still out in Canada.' That was hardly surprising, considering he never talked about his past life in his native country.

'Yes,' he said shortly, and added abruptly, 'Are you going to get into that damn bathroom, because I want to get to bed, even if you don't!'

'I was only asking about your relatives, not for intimate details of your love-life!' Jana flung at him as she walked swiftly out of the room.

The luxurious bathroom, with the exquisite tiling on both walls and floor and modern appointments, invited Jana to linger, tempted her to indulge in a long, hot soak in the deep bath. But, conscious that Kent was waiting, she stripped off her clothes quickly and made do with a cursory wash, promising herself a shower in the morning. She would rather have liked to wash out her underwear for the morning, but the thought of leaving her lacy bra and panties dripping over Kent's bath was embarrassing.

She borrowed his toothpaste, rubbing it over her teeth with a finger, deciding that her one luxury on a desert island would be a toothbrush. She glanced in the mirror above the basin to check that she didn't have toothpaste all over her chin, and stiffened as she saw the reflection of the bathroom door, from which hung a silky black négligé. Slowly she turned round, wondering why she hadn't noticed it sooner. Now that most certainly wasn't a present to Kent from his aunt in Canada. She tried to grin, but her lips wouldn't move. Well, she told herself briskly, she surely hadn't expected a man like Kent to be living like a monk? But she suddenly wished that the unknown female hadn't left quite such a blatant reminder of her presence.

She opened the door and, feeling acutely self-conscious in the huge shirt, walked awkwardly through into the living-room. Kent lifted his head from the book balanced on his knees and appraised her with a grin, and she wondered if she would ever get used to his rapid changes of mood. One moment he would be glowering at her and the next favouring her with a slow, lazy grin.

'Joseph and his coat of many colours. Suits you.' He stretched his arms wearily above his head and stood up. 'Everything you need?'

'Mmm.' She burrowed into the sheets on the converted sofa. 'Thanks, Kent. For everything,' she mumbled, gazing up into his face, totally unaware of how young and vulnerable she looked with the sheet drawn up under her chin, her eyes large and luminous.

He smiled, and moved across to the door.

Jana switched off the lamp behind her head and snuggled down more comfortably, hearing movements from the hall. Kent in the bathroom, Kent moving along to his bedroom. She closed her eyes quickly. She didn't want to think about Kent any more, didn't want to think about her flat, didn't want to think about anything. She willed herself to sleep, willed herself into an unconsciousness undisturbed by that recurring nightmare that sometimes made her terrified even to shut her eyes.

It was impossible. She was too restless, her mind too active. Swiftly, she flicked on the lamp and swung her legs on to the thick carpet. Fishing into her handbag, she retrieved the small bottle that she always kept with her, and padded quietly down the hall and into the kitchen.

She found a glass in one of the cupboards, filled it with water, shook out two tablets from the bottle and swallowed them.

'Headache? I heard you moving about . . .'

She jumped as she heard the deep voice behind her and swung round, her stomach muscles contracting at the sight of Kent in a white towelling robe. With an uneasy, disturbing twist of her heart she realised that he was not wearing pyjamas underneath, and quickly she averted her eyes from the unnerving expanse of tanned skin revealed by the robe, appalled to find herself wondering if the sheen of dark, matted hair ran the length of the hard chest.

'No, I haven't got a headache,' Jana heard herself mumble from a long way off. 'I couldn't sleep,' she explained, trying to look anywhere rather than at Kent, but he seemed to dominate the kitchen.

'Give me those!' Suddenly the bottle was wrenched from her hand, and Kent's face was above hers, white and tense with an emotion she couldn't begin to comprehend. 'Where the hell did you get these?' His eyes blazed into hers.

She stared at him, utterly bewildered by his anger. 'The doctor prescribed them for me after . . .' She broke off as he placed the small bottle in the pocket of his robe. 'Give those back to me. You have no right . . .' Her voice rose as swirling resentment engulfed her. He didn't suffer from those tortured nights—or did he? He was so self-contained it was impossible to know how he felt, but his loss had been as great as hers, Jana reminded herself guiltily. 'Kent, please give them back to me,' she repeated, trying to keep her voice calm, but it seemed to come out in a muffled choke. She was so tired, and so scared of sleeping, and a battle with Kent was just about the last straw. 'They're only mild sleeping-tablets,' she croaked, her eyes misting over with tears. She simply didn't seem to have the energy to go on fighting him.

The next moment she was encircled by a pair of strong arms, her head being pressed into the crook of a hard shoulder.

'I'm sorry, Jana. You were right. I shouldn't have

interfered.'

It was the unexpected gentleness in the gruff voice that was her undoing, made it impossible to hold back the tears that had been threatening all evening, any longer.

'I'm sorry,' she muttered chokingly. 'I'm making you wet.' She reached out a hand to wipe the tear-stained chest, and as her fingers touched the hard, bare skin, she was totally unprepared for the electric charge that surged up her arm, jolting her nerve-endings. Suddenly it was no longer comforting being held in that band of steel, but a whirlpool of alarming sensations. She could feel the warmth of the lean, taut body through her thin cotton shirt, was acutely conscious of the strong jawline, the square, decisive chin on a level somewhere above her head. The fragrance of clean, soapy male skin assailed her sense of smell, made her breathing erratic, sent the blood scalding through her veins.

Dazed, she tilted her face upwards, her eyes instantly locked into the dark, blue shadows. She lost all sense of time, there was nothing in the world but Kent; she could feel the warmth of his breath on her inflamed cheeks, see the hard, chiselled line of his mouth a few inches above hers. She couldn't stop that shiver running down her spine, an illogical feeling of near panic, almost of fear as the dark head came lower, towards her.

'Go to bed, Jana!'

The curt, dismissive words, the brusque, grating voice were as effective as a physical blow in shocking her out of her trance. She felt as if she had been douched with freezing water, aware that she was trembling as she stared up into eyes that had now changed to ice, his arms fallen to his sides.

'Go back to bed!' he repeated harshly and, turning away, strode out of the kitchen, leaving Jana staring after his retreating figure with dark, bewildered eyes.

Slowly, she walked back into the living-room. She sat on the side of the makeshift bed, staring into the darkness, and started to shudder again as she relived that moment of near panic when she had believed that Kent was going to kiss her, had almost tasted the hard mouth on hers. Her stomach lurched as she forced herself to acknowledge the truth. It hadn't been fear of Kent that had sent that cold shiver down her spine; she had been afraid of herself, of that swell of unexplored emotions that had suddenly been unleashed; terrified of that mounting desire that had surged up within her, forcing her to recognise her own latent sexuality for the first time.

She lay back on the bed and pulled the covers over her, thinking back to the boys she had dated during her year at college. Nice, uncomplicated young men who had made few emotional demands on her, who had been satisfied with brief, casual kisses. Kisses she had enjoyed, but which had made little impact, left her unmoved. Yet a few moments in Kent's arms had left her feeling weak and giddy, filled with a disturbing, aching longing.

Jana blinked open her eyes, disorientated for a second, and then she registered the sunlight pouring into the room between a gap in the cream curtains, and the sound of whistling coming from the bathroom. Kent. And it would appear that he was in a good mood.

She stretched her arms above her head and yawned. It was odd how things seemed so traumatic at night, and yet in the morning it was hard to believe they had ever happened, hard to remember those bewildering emotions that should have threatened her slumber. Yet she had fallen into a deep, dreamless sleep the moment her head had touched the pillow, the pills performing their usual magic.

The sharp peal of a bell cut through her lingering thoughts, and reluctantly she slipped out from the sheets and padded barefoot into the hall.

'Kent,' she called out. 'There's someone at the front door.'

'Well, answer it,' he bellowed back. 'I'm in the shower. It's probably the milkman for his money. Loose change on the kitchen table next to my wallet.'

The bellow made Jana grin, and any slight apprehension about facing Kent again after last night instantly vanished. He sounded so normal!

'I can't open the front door.' She thumped on the bathroom door. 'I'm not dressed.'

The door flew open and Kent's head and shoulders appeared around the corner. 'Don't you think this modesty bit is going too far?' he demanded. 'Put a sheet around you if you think the sight of your bare calves is going to send the milkman into a frenzy of unbridled passion.' His eyes suddenly gleamed. 'And I should do that button up.'

Jana followed his gaze to the gap in her shirt through which the swell of a small, firm breast was clearly revealed. Scarlet, she clutched the shirt to her.

'Now go and answer that door before I do it myself—and I'm warning you, I shan't bother with a robe.'

'Exhibitionist!' Jana muttered and fled.

She collected the change from the kitchen table, knocking Kent's wallet on to the floor in her haste, and made her way towards the front door, pulling a sheet off the bed and draping it around her shoulders, en route.

'Morning, love,' the milkman greeted her, taking hold of the money she proffered. 'Sorry to disturb you this early,' he added with a meaningful smile.

It was only when she had closed the door that Jana guessed at the automatic interpretation he must have put on her presence in Kent's flat, clad in a sheet, at that early hour of the morning. She started to grin. If only he knew how far from the truth his assumption had been. Not only had Kent been loath even to have her in the flat in the first place, but most of the time she doubted whether he even registered that she was female. Except perhaps for those brief, almost imperceptible seconds last night when he had held her in his arms, when she had witnessed that unguarded expression in the blue eyes. Deliberately, she cut off her thoughts, wary of the way they were heading.

She walked down the hall and into the kitchen, slightly taken aback to find Kent already there, filling up the kettle.

'Coffee?' he enquired, turning round to face her.

She nodded, trying to ignore the fact that he was once again clad in the white towelling robe, trying to ignore the sharp tang of recently applied expensive male aftershave, the dark hair, glistening with water, that sprang up waywardly around his head and made her suddenly long to curl her fingers through the rich thickness.

She fixed her eyes on the tiles above the sink. If she was forced to look at Kent for much longer she would become mesmerised.

'Look, I'll make the coffee while you dress,' she said with deceptive casualness. The glint in the blue eyes touched a nerve, gave rise to the uncomfortable suspicion that he was fully aware of the unnerving effect he was having on her. 'I'm not used to seeing half-naked men flaunting themselves about at breakfast-time,' she snapped, and instantly regretted it. But to her relief he didn't start teasing her, but merely nodded, turning towards the door.

'Oh, eggs on the top shelf.' He paused and grinned over his shoulder at her. 'And bacon in the fridge. I like mine crispy,' he added enthusiastically, and sounded so much like a ravenous schoolboy that Jana couldn't help smiling, beginning to relax.

'Huh!' She pretended indignation. 'I suppose this is where you think women belong, in the kitchen—and don't say it. It's unoriginal,' she finished off quickly, deciding she had walked right into that one.

She felt curiously light-headed as she bustled around the kitchen, examining all the cupboards to find the necessary utensils. It was nice not to be on her own on a Saturday morning, she thought with a rush of contentment—and especially nice, she admitted with reluctant honesty, to be with Kent.

She set the bacon on a low heat, humming under her breath, and then out of the corner of her eye, she saw the wallet lying under the table where it had fallen earlier. She stooped to retrieve it, noticing that something had fallen out of the leather case. Frowning, she picked up the small, white square of card and turned it over in her hand. A girl of about her own age, with soft brown eyes, laughed up at her. It took her a full minute to start resenting the fact that

Kent carried a picture in his wallet of one of the most beautiful girls she had ever seen, and another two minutes to admit it to herself. Exactly what she resented, she refused to analyse, refused to acknowledge the logical reason for that knot in her stomach.

She stared down at the photograph. There was an innocence in the large, brown eyes, a suggestion of vulnerability about the curved mouth that puzzled her. This girl didn't look Kent's type—or at least not how she had always imagined the type of woman Kent would be attracted to, sophisticated, assured, experienced.

'Breakfast ready?'

She spun round, annoyed to find that she felt guilty, as if she had been caught prying. With forced nonchalance she held out the photograph. 'Fell out of your wallet.'

She watched as Kent took the snapshot from her in silence, and pushed it deep into the pocket of his jeans.

'Who is she?' she asked with studied unconcern. It would be pointless to pretend she hadn't even looked at the photograph. She saw the familiar, shuttered expression drop over the dark face and knew that the best course of action would be to let the matter drop, but she couldn't stop herself.

'She's very pretty,' she commented casually, not expecting any verbal response from Kent, but hoping that just for once he would let the mask slip, that he would give some indication, however slight, of exactly how much the unknown girl meant to him.

'She was beautiful.' The harsh brittleness in his voice cut through Jana like a razor. 'She's dead.'

CHAPTER THREE

JANA went cold, rigid, staring unseeingly down at the floor. She felt chilled to the core, numb, as she had felt after her mother's death. She raised her head and was further shocked when, for a brief, imperceptible second, she glimpsed the raw, naked emotion on Kent's face, the deep searing pain in his dark eyes. She wondered how she could have ever supposed that he was incapable of any depth of feeling, incapable of suffering.

She felt sick. For a few moments she had been jealous of that girl with the vivacious, glowing face . . . and that girl was dead.

'Kent, I'm so sorry,' she said unsteadily. The words sounded inadequate, but they were all she had to offer.

He made no response, but with a movement as definite as slamming a door in her face straddled a stool by the table and opened the morning newspaper.

Jana turned back to the stove and broke an egg mechanically into the pan, acutely conscious of the silent figure physically just a few feet away, but mentally she knew not where. Her eyes, green pools of uncertainty and compassion, rested on the bowed, dark head and her stomach lurched. She felt so hopeless. She was powerless to help him; he would never confide in her, never seek comfort in her arms as she had in his. There was nothing she could do to breach that wall guarding his innermost emotions and

51

thoughts.

'We'd better get your locks changed first thing after breakfast.' He spoke for the first time as she handed him a plate.

'Yes.' She nodded, only conscious of the dull ache inside her.

Jana stood guard over the luggage, watching Kent move assuredly across the terminal to the car rental desk, and heaved a deep sigh. He had barely said more than two words to her on the flight over; in fact, she thought ruefully, he had hardly spoken to her for the last three weeks. He had been out of the office much of the time, relaying his orders to her via the dictaphone, and on the few occasions they had encountered each other their conversation had been reduced to essentials, his manner cool and distant.

Her eyes rested on the dark head clearly visible above the throng of people, and she wondered sadly if he was regretting having asked her on this trip in the first place. He looked as cool and as alert as when they had boarded the aircraft at Heathrow all those hours ago, Jana mused, whereas she felt a wreck. Hot, sticky and decidedly travel-worn, even though she had tried to freshen up before landing.

The lemon suit with the straight, close-fitting skirt and her matching high-heeled court shoes hadn't been the most comfortable of travel wear. She would have felt a lot happier in her more practical denims, but, having read somewhere that airlines refused passengers wearing jeans entry into their first-class section, she had regretfully opted for the smart suit.

Then when Kent had collected her in the taxi en

route to the airport she had been irritated to discover that he was dressed casually in jeans and a blue shirt. But then, Jana had decided wryly, it would have to be a brave girl on the check-in desk who told Kent that he couldn't travel in his denims.

She lost sight of him and gazed around the busy terminal, intrigued by the checked shirts, high-heeled boots and cowboy hats worn by many of the men, wondering if this was their habitual wear or had been prompted by the impending Stampede. She liked listening to their drawling voices, their accents more pronounced than Kent's, but then he had spent most of the last thirteen years in England. Not for the first time, she wondered why he had left his native country at twenty-one.

'All right?' she asked rhetorically as he came striding back towards her, noting with a certain amount of relief the car keys he held in his hand. She had been responsible for arranging their itinerary, reserving their flight seats and the hire car, booking their first night's accommodation in a hotel in downtown Calgary. Tomorrow Kent was going to see Ben Sinclair to check that there were no last-minute snags, and then they were driving to Jasper and staying on a campsite run by friends of Kent's, Jake and Cindy Stewart.

What she had done to deserve this short holiday Jana still didn't know, but she had decided not to look a gift-horse in the mouth. If Kent had an ulterior motive for bringing her to Canada he still hadn't enlightened her, and his off-hand manner over the last few weeks had dissuaded her from asking.

She flicked him a glance out of the corner of her eye as they walked silently out into the sunshine and raised her small chin defiantly. Whatever happened, even if Kent practically ignored her the whole time they were in Canada, she was determined to enjoy herself.

Kent drove skilfully through the traffic which became increasingly heavy as they neared the city, adapting effortlessly to the right side of the road.

Jana stared out of the window and admitted to a small twinge of disappointment. Calgary at first sight looked just like one more city in the rush hour. But then, she decided honestly, she probably wasn't being fair. Right then nothing would appear enticing, except a hot bath and a comfortable bed. The clock on the dashboard might claim it was only five o'clock, but her body knew that it was a lie, that it was really midnight. Unsuccessfully, she tried to stifle a yawn.

'That boring?' Kent enquired, his eyes never straying from the road, lean brown hands gripped firmly around the steering-wheel.

'It's all right for you,' she retorted a little waspishly. 'You slept practically the whole way. You didn't even bother with the meals.' They had been delicious, Jana recalled.

'I think you ate enough for both of us,' he commented drily.

She shot a glance at the craggy profile. So he hadn't really been asleep, just pretending. To avoid talking to her? she wondered ruefully. She looked back out of the window and found it impossible to imagine the parade that heralded the start of the Stampede ever managing to make its way unhindered through the congested city centre. Or did Calgary simply come to a standstill for two hours?

Evidently familiar with the city, Kent had no need

to consult the map provided by the car rental firm, locating the large modern hotel situated down one of the many avenues that crossed the centre street from west to east with ease. ·

The fair-headed girl behind the reception desk in the plush hotel foyer greeted them with a wide, friendly smile.

'Reservation in the name of Tyson.' Kent smiled back. It was the first time she had seen him smile for days, Jana realised with a sharp pang, and then it had to be at another girl.

The receptionist studied the book in front of her and nodded. 'Mr and Mrs Tyson. Suite on the third floor. If you'd like to register here, sir.'

'But . . .' Jana gasped, but before the words of protest could form in her startled mouth, Kent had intervened smoothly.

'I think there must be some error. We have two separate bookings. Tyson and Morton.'

The girl frowned and scanned the register again. 'I'm sorry sir, but we only have the one reservation.'

'Kent, I did not make a mistake,' Jana muttered through clenched teeth. She recalled making the booking so clearly: a suite for Kent and a smaller room for herself; remembered being intrigued by the fact that the hotel had non-smoking floors, cable television in all the rooms and en suite 'washrooms' with 'tubs' as well as showers. 'I've got the telex confirmation somewhere.' Back home in England.

The receptionist listened with a polite smile, taking in every detail of the tall, dark-haired man, the expression in her eyes clearly stating that if Jana had made a mistake it had been intentional and who could blame her.

'I'm afraid I can't offer you any alternative accommodation. The hotel's full.' She gazed up at Kent appreciatively. 'I don't think you'll find anywhere else, sir. The city's chock-a-block right now with Stampede coming up.'

Kent drew Jana to one side. 'It doesn't appear that we have much choice.'

She looked up into his grim face and her heart sank. This was most definitely not the most auspicious of starts to their trip. 'Look, I didn't make a . . .' she started again, but he cut through with a sigh.

'Give it a rest, Jana, for goodness' sake,' he said curtly, making her feel like a petulant child, and strode back to sign the register.

The suite was larger than Jana's own flat in London. Beside the bedroom and bathroom, there was a living-room and dining-area, with a kitchen tucked into a small alcove.

She stood in the middle of the light, airy living-room with its plush furnishings and carpet and surveyed Kent as he stood by the window, gazing out over the towering city buildings. He hadn't said one word during their brief inspection of the spacious suite, but his grim face had dispelled Jana's optimism that sharing the hotel rooms with Kent wouldn't be so very different from staying in his flat.

'You'd better take the bedroom,' he said brusquely without turning round.

'Thanks.' She refused to feel guilty because he had elected to spend an uncomfortable night on the sofa, conscious only of relief that as soon as the porter brought up their luggage, she could retreat into the bedroom and close the door on Kent.

If only he would make some flippant remark she

would feel easier, but his continuing silence set her teeth on edge. She looked across the room at the daunting broad back and wanted to scream. It was like being in a room with a total stranger, the tension almost unbearable. She took a deep calming breath.

'Kent, if you're furious with me, say so and let's get it over and done with,' she muttered. 'I can't stand it when you're . . .'

'What?' he enquired icily, swinging round to face her.

'Oh, don't look at me like that!' she snapped. 'This is far worse for me than you. I mean, at least you're probably used to sharing with . . . er . . . someone,' she faltered.

His eyes narrowed to chilling blue slits. 'I can assure you that this is a totally new experience for me too.' With swift strides he moved across the room and flung open the door in response to the porter's knock, leaving Jana in no doubt as to what was new about the situation for him.

Thankfully, she picked up her suitcase and retreated into the bedroom, the cream and gold décor giving a pleasing illusion of reflected sunlight. She kicked off her shoes and wiggled her feet in the deep carpet, and eyed the large, comfortable-looking bed. She would shower and unpack later, she decided quickly. All she wanted to do right now was stretch out on that inviting bed and close her eyes.

She slipped off her jacket, sat down on the edge of her bed and then sighed as she heard Kent's voice.

'Come in,' she said reluctantly and looked up enquiringly as he filled the doorway.

'Did you bring a swimsuit with you?' he demanded.

'Yes,' she murmured cautiously, frowning at the

abrupt question.

'Good. Because we're going swimming.'

'Now?' She eyed him in disbelief. '*We* most certainly are not!' She stressed the pronoun. 'But thanks for asking,' she added sweetly. 'What is all this anyway? Are you on some sort of keep-fit, health kick?'

'Exercise is the best antidote for jet-lag,' he told her crisply. 'And I don't want you yawning your head off for the next two days!'

'OK, I'll go for a jog round the block later if it makes you happy,' she said witheringly. She flopped back on the bed to make it quite clear that she considered her remedy for jet-lag infinitely superior to his, and then gave out a startled gasp as she was firmly yanked off the bed and on to her feet.

'Get your swimsuit now,' he ordered her quietly.

She stared up at him, eyes dark with mounting resentment. 'In case you weren't aware of it,' she said sarcastically, 'it's the middle of the night right now in England, and well after six o'clock here—so either way, I'm off duty.'

She didn't trust that tight-lipped smile.

'While you're over here with me,' he said coolly, 'you're on duty when I say and for as long as I say. See you in the pool in five minutes. Basement floor.'

Before she had had time even to think of a retort, he had closed the door firmly behind him.

'Damn you, Kent Tyson!' Jana gave vent to her feelings and then, scowling, walked over to her suitcase. She had no doubt that if she failed to put in an appearance at the pool Kent would be quite capable of coming back up to fetch her, and she had no wish to be dragged forcibly down the corridor like an errant child.

She stripped off her clothes and pulled on her dark red swimsuit, and then frowned as she caught sight of her reflection in the full-length mirror on the door of the fitted wardrobe. Either she had put on weight since she had bought the costume last summer, or it had shrunk. It now clung to her like a second skin, moulding itself to the firm, small breasts, outlining every contour of her slim body. Neither could she remember it being cut quite so high on the legs. She shrugged. Oh, well, it couldn't be helped, and anyway, Kent wasn't likely to give her more than a brief, cursory glance. She pulled a cream sweatshirt over her head and tugged on her jeans.

The swimming-pool was empty except for the one solitary swimmer, cutting through the water with effortless ease. Unobserved, Jana stood for a second in the shadow on the changing-room door, a lump forming in her throat at the sheer beauty of the sleek, powerful male form.

He reached the far end of the pool, and as he pulled himself out Jana sucked in her breath unsteadily, colour staining her cheeks, totally unprepared for the effect of that bronzed, almost naked masculine body.

Droplets of water gleamed on the broad, bare shoulders, glistened on the mat of fine dark hair that covered the muscular chest, tapered down over the taut, flat stomach and disappeared beneath the waistband of the black swimming-trunks. As he executed a perfect dive back into the pool, Jana walked quickly to the edge and slipped in, the water cool on her heated skin.

With jerky, ungainly movements of her legs and arms, she ploughed slowly down the pool, keeping her head held high above the waterline. By the time she had reached the far end, Kent had lapped her three times, and sat casually on the side, long, lean legs dangling into the water.

She clung to the edge, breathlessly, surprised at how relaxed Kent looked, all trace of tension vanished, a broad grin softening his harsh features. She felt the familiar sense of bewilderment at the rapid mood-change. It was hard to believe that this man looking down at her, blue eyes glinting with ill-concealed amusement, was the same man who only a short time ago had appraised her with cold indifference. Impossible, too, to recall her fierce resentment at the high-handed way he had ordered her to the pool.

'What's so funny?' she demanded with pretended indignation, having no illusions about her prowess in the water. How weak she was, she thought with sudden self-disgust as she glanced up into the tanned face. Kent had only to smile at her like that and she seemed to forget all her grievances, forget how infuriating he could be, was only conscious of a warm rush of fluttering happiness. Still, she consoled herself quickly, life would become remarkably complicated if she harboured a grudge against Kent every time he spoke harshly to her, or issued one of his imperial commands.

'Do you always swim with your nose in the air?' he enquired teasingly.

'I have a very individual style which it has taken me years to perfect,' she said airily and then grinned back at him. 'Well, at least I can get from A to B.'

'As long as A to B isn't more than twenty yards or so?' He raised a dark, sceptical eyebrow at her.

She refused to be baited any longer and, taking a deep breath, pushed off from the wall. She had only covered a couple of yards when Kent caught up with her, swimming alongside easily, surveying her strenuous but largely ineffectual efforts with bright, critical blue eyes.

'Try and keep your body flat,' he advised her. 'You're putting too much effort into it. Relax.'

Relax! Jana absorbed the command with wry amusement. How could she relax with that alarming male presence only a few feet away?

He continued to bark instructions at her until finally both her patience and her limbs were exhausted. She was here, against her will, for a quiet, peaceful swim—not to be badgered unmercifully like this.

'Are you a frustrated swimming-coach or something? I'm not in training for the Olympics,' she said ungratefully, and then spluttered as she swallowed a mouthful of water. She floundered to a halt, her legs floating down underneath her, misjudged the depth of the pool, and was submerged under the water. She bobbed to the surface, gasping for air, and then her gasp changed to one of shock as she was lifted above the water, her head on a level with Kent's.

'Put me down,' she protested, her small breasts rising and falling in time with her erratic breathing, her hands automatically reaching out for the damp, gleaming shoulders to steady herself. Her eyes darkened with agitation as she became conscious of those firm hands resting on her slender hips, of her legs floating against the hair-roughened ones as Kent moved towards the edge of the pool.

'Put me . . .'

The words choked in her throat as the hard
warm mouth covered her parted lips, stunning her
into silence. Her head reeled at the unexpected
onslaught of her senses, aware of the pressure of
Kent's hand on her back curving her body into his
hard, lean form.

Her mind urged her to pull away, but she seemed
powerless to obey, didn't want to obey, only conscious
of that spiral of languorous, sensual pleasure, her
arms reaching up instinctively around his neck, her
fingers curling into the thick, dark hair.

As he lifted his head, she felt bereft, empty, filled
with an aching, unsatisfied longing.

'Kent,' she murmured his name, looking into his
face with dazed, dark green eyes.

'You're shivering,' he said abruptly. 'Get
dressed.'

Before she had time to register what was happening
she found herself deposited none too gently on the
side of the pool, and Kent was swimming away with
long, powerful strokes.

Without hesitation, Jana scrambled to her feet and,
breathing unsteadily, walked swiftly towards the
changing-rooms. She opened her locker to retrieve her
clothes and then, as she turned round and glimpsed
her reflection in the wall mirror, she stiffened,
appalled as she saw the hardened nipples clearly
outlined beneath the damp nylon swimsuit. Soft
colour flooded her cheeks at the humiliating
knowledge that a brief, casual kiss from Kent
could arouse such a tangible physical response in
her.

She had no illusions that the spur-of-the-moment
kiss had been as meaningless to him as a cup of coffee,
had no doubts that he had already dismissed it from

his mind. And if she had any sense at all, she would do the same.

She turned on the shower and stepped under the heated water and suddenly wished despairingly that it was as easy to erase the memory of that hard mouth and the lean, strong body from her thoughts as it was to soap off the scent of chlorine from her skin.

She hung her swimsuit over the bath to dry as soon as she returned to the suite, and then spent a few moments unpacking the clothes she would need for the morning, hanging up a blue cotton dress in the wardrobe. How long would Kent be? she wondered, her ears tuned for the sound of his key in the outer door.

Restlessly, she wandered back into the living-room and slumped down into one of the comfortable armchairs, idly picking up the courtesy Alberta information pack from the adjacent table.

Her interest quickened as she spread open a map and pored over it. Kent had already told her the route they would be taking tomorrow, the Trans Canada Highway to Banff, then on to Jasper through the parkway. She couldn't suppress that mounting anticipation. There were so many places she wanted to see: Lake Louise, the Athabascar Glacier, the Columbia Icefield. Would Kent make a few detours if she asked him? She shook her head ruefully, knowing that she wouldn't even bother to ask. He was so unpredictable. He might acquiesce with a lazy, teasing grin—but on the other hand he was just as likely to refuse her tentative request with a curt, dismissive shake of his head.

She heaved a deep sigh. Was he by nature prone to those swift, inexplicable changes of mood? Or was it something fundamental in her character that irked him, rubbed him up the wrong way and triggered off those cold, caustic comments? She frowned. She used not to have that effect on him, she mused reflectively, thinking back to the days when she had first come to London, to those lazy Sunday afternoons they had spent together exploring London. In those days he had treated her with amused tolerance, teasing her relentlessly, but she hadn't minded—at least, not at first. It was only when she had come to realise that she was merely a duty to him that the pleasure in his company had vanished.

Her eyes clouded. No, it wasn't until she had started to work for Kent, seen him five days a week, that she had been subjected to his erratic, explosive moods. She smiled wryly. Perhaps the explanation was obvious; simply a case of familiarity breeding contempt, or, in Kent's case, cold intolerance.

Her body tensed as she heard his key in the door and she was acutely conscious of his eyes resting on her as he strode into the room. For one uncomfortable second she thought he was going to refer to that brief episode in the pool, and she was overwhelmingly grateful when he merely announced that he was hungry and walked over to his suitcase.

She realised how right she had been in her assessment of his indifferent response to that kiss, and wished longingly that she could discard the memory of Kent's mouth on hers so easily, but it remained indelibly impressed on her mind. What on earth was the matter with her? She pulled herself up sharply. She was behaving like an over-emotional adolescent who had been kissed for the first time. Anyone would think Kent had taken her by force and made love to her from the way she was reacting, she told herself crisply. But instead of restoring her sense of proportion, as was intended, the traitorous thought conjured up mental images that burned her face fiery red.

Quickly she bowed her head, pretending to be absorbed in the map until the colour had receded from her cheeks. Under the shielding dark lashes, she watched Kent unlock his suitcase and pull out a navy blue shirt.

'Do you want to go out to eat or shall we have something sent up?' he asked casually over his shoulder.

'Let's go out,' Jana said quickly. The thought of sharing an intimate meal with Kent in the suite was unnerving; neither, she suddenly realised, did she want to eat in the formal hotel dining-room. 'Do you know what I really feel like?' She eyed him cautiously. 'Junk food.'

She could have cried with relief as he grinned at her. 'A great big, juicy hamburger with all the trimmings?'

'And a huge pile of chips,' she smiled back, tension easing from her.

'Ask for fries or you'll end up with a plate of potato crisps,' he advised her, and frowned thoughtfully. 'When I was last over here a couple of years ago, there was this particularly good hamburger joint about four blocks away.'

'I feel like a walk,' Jana responded quickly, suddenly aching to be out in the fresh air.

'Right.' He nodded, rubbing a lean hand over the dark stubble on his chin. 'I'll just have a quick shave and change my shirt.' To her relief he headed towards the bathroom. For one moment, she had thought that he intended changing his shirt in front of her—and she had seen quite enough bronzed, male skin for one day.

She darted into the bedroom and emerged a few minutes later, deciding that with freshly brushed hair, a touch of lipstick and clad in her favourite denims, she could cope with anything, even Kent.

The hamburger was every bit as good as he had promised, Jana thought with satisfaction, wiping ketchup from her face.

'I don't know where you put it all,' Kent studied her slight figure with mock bewilderment.

'You can talk,' she returned indignantly. 'I only had one and a bit. You had two and finished off the rest of mine.' She took a sip of strawberry milk shake and decided that it was a bit sickly on top of the huge hamburger and she might have been wiser to stick to black coffee like Kent.

'Anything else?' he asked solicitously. 'A double portion of pecan pie?'

'I'm not that much of a pig,' she told him with a grin. 'Just a little one.' She sat back in her chair and sighed contentedly, feeling more relaxed with Kent than she had been for weeks. If only their relationship could always be this easy and undemanding, she thought wistfully, and then smiled up at him. He looked so cramped in the small eating-booth, without the space to stretch out his long legs.

'Right, if you're sure you've had enough, I'll get the bill.' As Kent reached into his pocket, Jana delved into her purse and pushed a pile of silver coins across the table to him.

'Here's my half.'

He looked up startled. 'I told you this is an all-expenses-paid trip.' He broke into a lazy grin. 'Still, if you insist on throwing your money about, you can buy me a doughnut on the way back to the hotel.'

'What? And you call me a pig!' Jana demanded, a rush of happiness sweeping through her.

It was cooler outside, night falling, but the darkness was kept at bay by the glow of the neon signs from the restaurants and bars and the illuminated displays of the huge department stores.

With a sudden, inexplicable pang, Jana noticed a young couple ahead of them on the pavement, sauntering along hand in hand. As she and Kent walked briskly by them, she couldn't resist turning her head, registering with a twinge of envy how happy they looked, how totally absorbed in each other's company.

She stole a glance up at the man beside her, seeing as if for the first time the harsh planes beneath the jutting cheekbones, the uncompromising angle of the square, resolute chin, the lines of cynicism etched around the straight, hard mouth. It was impossible to imagine Kent ever being totally preoccupied with any one woman; he might take them out, take them to bed, but he would never allow them to enter his life. Jana's stomach suddenly turned over, remembering the photograph in his wallet. Perhaps once, Kent had needed someone.

'Mr Tyson?'

The same receptionist was on duty when they walked into the hotel foyer. Jana wondered a little caustically if she remembered the name of every guest in the hotel so easily and tried to ignore the tightening of her stomach muscles as she saw the way Kent was smiling down into the inviting eyes.

'There was a telephone message for you, sir. Mr Jameson. He left a message.'

Jana waited until Kent had read the message card

and then walked with him across to the
elevator.

'We've a breakfast appointment tomorrow,' he told
her quietly, pressing the call button.

'With Mr Jameson? Who is he? A business
associate?' she asked without a great deal of interest.
Her relaxed mood of wellbeing had evaporated
without warning, and she began to feel strangely edgy
as they reached the third floor and walked down the
landing.

'You might say that,' Kent answered eventually,
and Jana frowned at the odd note of reluctance in his
voice, but was in no mood to delve further.

He unlocked the door of the suite and stood aside,
allowing her to enter first. Then abruptly he
thrust the door-keys back in his pocket and turned
away.

'You go to bed. I'm going back down for a nightcap
in the bar.'

'What?' Jana demanded but it was too late. The
door had closed and she could hear Kent's footsteps
fading down the corridor.

'Wonderful!' she muttered sarcastically, walking
into the bedroom and flinging her handbag down on
the bed, registering that the chambermaid had been in
to turn down the covers.

Kent had deposited her back in the suite as neatly
as if she had been an unwanted parcel and now
gone . . . where? She scowled. Did that pretty
receptionist just happen to come off duty about now?
She shook herself mentally. She had no claim on
Kent; he was free to do whatever he wanted and she
had no right to mind.

Jana came out of the bathroom clad in the T-shirt
she used as a nightdress, wishing that it hadn't shrunk

quite so much last time she had washed it, and that she had thought to bring a dressing-gown with her. But then, she hadn't been anticipating company in her hotel rooms.

How long was Kent going to be? She prowled around the bedroom, discovered a spare blanket in one of the wardrobes, picked up a pillow from the bed, and, carrying them through to the living-room, deposited them on the sofa.

Jana seemed to be awake the whole night, staring up into the darkness, listening for Kent's return. Where was he, and who was he with? The questions tore into her brain and the answers that presented themselves made her clench her small fists in silent protest. But she must have fallen into a fitful doze eventually because suddenly she was being shaken gently on the shoulder and Kent was standing by the bed, a cup of tea in his left hand.

'I did knock,' he said quietly, 'but you were dead to the world. We're meeting Andrew Jameson in twenty minutes.'

'Go away, Kent,' Jana muttered peevishly, never at her best first thing in the morning. All she wanted to do was close her eyes and go back to sleep. 'I'll skip breakfast,' she murmured, turning on to her side. 'I'm sure you and Mr Jameson can manage without my scintillating after-breakfast conversation.'

'Jana, get up. Now.'

The warning note in his voice made her sit up. She had no wish to be dragged unceremoniously from her bed, clad only in her skimpy T-shirt. She focused her eyes on him for the first time, registering that he was already dressed in the formal grey suit in preparation for his meeting with Ben Sinclair later on that morning. So he must have come back to the suite eventually last night, though judging from those lines of weariness on his face he had spent not only a short night but an uncomfortable one on the sofa.

'Sleep all right?' he enquired almost as an afterthought as he moved to the door.

'Like a log,' Jana said cheerfully, determined that he would never know of those long hours she had lain awake listening for him.

'See you downstairs in about a fifteen minutes,' he said crisply, closing the door behind him.

She waited until she heard him leave the suite and then slipped from the bed and darted into the living-room. Despising herself, she moved swiftly across to the sofa and stared down at it. The blanket and pillow lay undisturbed, exactly where she had placed them last night. She had been wrong—Kent hadn't slept on the sofa after all. He must have come back early this morning to wash and change. So where had he spent last night? a voice clamoured in her head. Did he just happen to have an old girlfriend still living in Calgary? The brittle, tearing sensation that cramped her stomach muscles was so intense, so unexpected that she almost cried out with shock, filled with self-disgust that she should be such an easy victim to one of the most destructive of all the emotions. An emotion, she told herself fiercely as she headed towards the bathroom, that she had no justification for feeling.

She slipped on the blue cotton dress and brushed her hair vigorously. It was growing at long last, and, damp from the shower, formed waves around her face. Without much enthusiasm, she inspected herself in the mirror and applied a light touch of red lip-gloss.

Her flawless skin looked unnaturally pale, but she knew from past experience that too much blusher made her look like a painted doll. Her eyes were dull and lifeless, with dark, purple shadows underneath, betraying her restless night. Weren't eyes supposed to be the windows of the soul? Jana frowned. No one, especially not Kent, was going to glimpse her soul today, or those confused, disturbing thoughts.

Kent was standing outside the dining-room, talking to a tall, thin, dark-suited man in his early forties, but as soon as he saw Jana he broke off his conversation abruptly, and both men turned to face her.

It was rather daunting, she decided, to have two men watching her so intently as she walked across the foyer towards them.

Before either of them could say a word, she smiled and touched the huge red-rimmed sunglasses that dominated her small face.

'I've woken up with a headache,' she explained airily, ignoring Kent's forbidding frown completely. It wasn't a complete fabrication; her head did feel heavy, but that curious ache was more in the region of her heart, she acknowledged despondently.

'Cute!' Kent drawled, his face like thunder, and turned to the man by his side. 'Andrew Jameson,' his mouth tightened, 'and this is Jana, Jana Morton.'

'How do you do, Mr Jameson,' she said politely, deciding that she hadn't much cared for the way Kent had made her sound like some sort of infectious disease. She took hold of the extended hand, slightly taken aback to find that it trembled in her slight grip. She didn't usually have an unnerving effect on men.

She looked into the thin face curiously, noting that the gentle brown eyes were gazing back at her with shy concentration.

'Right, shall we go in?' Kent said shortly, pushing open the glass doors. A hovering waitress showed them immediately to a white-clothed table at the far end of the spacious dining-room.

Jana ordered pancakes simply because the two men selected them. She didn't feel hungry in the least, but to refuse breakfast would instantly alert Kent.

She watched in silent amazement the relish with which both men devoured their food, liberally doused with maple syrup, and forced herself to swallow her own. She was finding it increasingly difficult to keep that fixed smile on her lips, and impossible to concentrate on the light conversation that passed between the two men.

'And what do you think of our country so far?'

She recollected herself quickly, realising that Andrew Jameson had directed the question to her.

'I haven't seen a great deal yet,' she didn't have to force the enthusiasm into her voice, 'but I'm really looking forward to seeing the Rockies. And hopefully the Stampede next week.' She shot a quick glance at Kent as she said that, not having yet established that she would have the free time to wander around the Stampede grounds.

'When I get back from Ottawa on Thursday, perhaps you and Kent would like to come and look around the ranch.'

Jana jerked her head upwards. What ranch? She really should have been paying more attention instead of letting her thoughts fly off at those uncomfortable tangents.

'I'd love to come,' she murmured and then deciding that something else was called for, added vaguely, 'It must be wonderful being a cowboy, working out of doors all day. All those wide-open spaces . . . and cows and things.' Even to her own ears she sounded ridiculous.

'Er—yes.'

She wasn't surprised that he looked so nonplussed, and it suddenly occurred to her that Andrew Jameson was the last person she would have imagined to be a rancher. He didn't have the air of a man used to hard, physical work, battling against the elements each day. Now Kent, she decided, automatically flicking him a glance, she could easily visualise in that role.

She turned her attention back to the older man, studying him thoughtfully as he started talking to Kent again. There was something oddly familiar about the long, sensitive face, the unassuming gentleness in his eyes. She shook her head mentally. No, she couldn't think who he reminded her of, and then, aware that he had risen to his feet, she smiled up at him.

'I must go. My plane,' he murmured apologetically, glancing at his wristwatch.

Kent stood up and shook his hand. 'I'll bring Jana over to the Flying J. on Thursday then.'

'Goodbye, Mr Jameson,' Jana murmured courteously, and watched him walk across the dining-room with jerky strides, slightly puzzled by the way so many heads turned round as he passed their tables.

'Did you discuss business before I came down?' she asked abruptly as Kent sat down again.

'Sorry?' He gave her a sharp look. 'Take off those ridiculous glasses. You look like a mini Elton John.'

'I like them,' she said defiantly, smiling her acceptance as the waitress offered to refill her coffee-cup, and then watched in silent amazement as Kent poured cream into his own replete cup.

'What did you think of Andrew?'

'He seemed very pleasant,' she murmured without much interest and couldn't stop herself from exclaiming, 'You've just put sugar into your coffee as well as cream!'

'What?' He didn't seem in the least concerned, simply frowned at his cup and pushed it to one side. 'So you liked him, then?'

'Liked him?' Jana echoed, baffled. 'I only spoke to the man about twice. How do I know if I liked him?' Her eyes narrowed. 'What is all this, Kent? What does it matter what I think of Andrew?' She didn't trust that uncharacteristic, cagey expression on his face. He was up to something, she was convinced of it.

He looked at her directly. 'Have you any idea of who he is?'

'Should I?' she demanded irritably. 'Do I get a prize for the right answer?' Her face cleared as something clicked in her brain. 'Yes, I do know,' she announced triumphantly. 'He's *the* Andrew Jameson, isn't he? The writer. I saw him on a TV chat show.' She smiled. 'I remember especially because he looked as if he was being tortured and I couldn't understand why he'd ever agreed to do the interview in the first place.' She shook her head wonderingly. 'You'd never think to look at him that he'd written all those thrillers.' She glanced at the silent man opposite her enquiringly. 'How do you know him, Kent?'

'I've known him for years,' he said quietly. 'Oh, hell, there's no easy way to tell you this, Jana. Andrew is your father.'

CHAPTER FOUR

'WHAT?' Jana's face burnt with angry colour. 'If this is some sort of joke, it's sick!' She snatched the dark glasses from her face without even being aware of doing so and then, as her green eyes glared into the blue ones, she went ashen.

'I don't believe you,' she said numbly, but she was only paying lip-service to the words, had read the truth in those brilliant eyes. So many questions hammered in her head but she seemed to be unable to think straight.

'Why didn't he tell me himself?' she finally blurted out in a high-pitched voice.

Kent's eyes did not waver from her stricken face. 'He couldn't,' he answered simply.

'How long have you known that he was . . . my father?' she asked in a small, bewildered voice.

'Always,' he admitted. 'Don't forget your mother worked for my father in Calgary, and she never made any secret about her relationship with Andrew.'

'You've known all this time and never told me?' Jana felt sick with shuddering fury.

'Your mother asked me not . . .' he began quietly, but she wasn't listening, couldn't concentrate on his words, aware only of an emotion, too confusing to analyse, that gnawed deep into her, and overrode the sense of shock.

'You arranged the whole thing. This was why you asked me to come to Canada with you, wasn't it?' Her voice rose accusingly.

'Come on, let's get out of here,' Kent said forcefully. 'I'm not meeting Ben for an hour. We'll take a walk and sort this out.'

'Thanks very much,' she flung back bitterly. 'You can fit me in for an hour between appointments.' She took a deep, gulping breath. 'Well, I don't want to talk to you. I don't want to go anywhere with you. I want to go back to England. Right now.'

'Calm down, Jana,' he murmured quietly, stretching out an arm across the table.

She shook off his restraining hand and leapt to her feet.

'I'm so sorry, Kent,' she spat out caustically. 'I'm being over-emotional.' Her voice shook. 'Next time someone casually informs me out of the blue that some stranger is my father, I'll try and deal with it more rationally.'

'Try and understand, Jana.' His voice was low and intense.

'Understand what? That someone I . . . trusted set me up?' Her eyes darkened with hurt and anger. 'Go and see Ben. Go to hell for all I care. Just leave me alone.' Blindly, she headed for the door, not knowing or caring where she was going, just wanting desperately to get as far away from Kent as possible.

Jana stared listlessly out of the car window, eyes squinting against the glare of the midday sun, remembering too late that she had left her dark glasses on the hotel dining-room table all those hours ago. They were heading west, away from Calgary.

'Look over to your left.' Kent broke the silence as he drove steadily along the highway. 'Through the clouds. Your first glimpse of the Rockies.'

The mountain peaks became more discernible and,

despite that knotted, confused feeling inside her, Jana couldn't stop the swirl of anticipation, but for some perverse reason she was determined not to show her excitement to Kent, and remained silent and deadpan.

'We'll stop off for lunch in Banff and then, if you like, take a quick trip over to Lake Louise before going on.'

'Stop humouring me,' she snapped. 'I'm not a child.'

'Well, stop behaving like a spoilt brat, then,' he retorted brusquely, the tight line of his square jaw showing how close he was to losing his temper.

She lowered her eyes. He was right, she was acting like a sulky child. Her mouth twisted wryly, knowing that something deep inside her had been quite deliberately building up a festering resentment against Kent, because that blocked out all other, more painful emotions.

When she had stormed out of the hotel early that morning, she had pounded the pavements until her feet ached, totally oblivious to her surroundings. By the time she'd managed to find her way back to the hotel, she had worked off her initial shock and had felt calmer, more in control of herself, had believed she was now prepared to face Kent with equanimity.

He had been sitting in the living-room, already changed from his suit into jeans and a shirt.

'Are you all right?' he had demanded immediately she had walked in, frowning his concern. 'Want to talk?' he'd added gently.

Jana had looked at him, and that twisted feeling of animosity had stirred again.

'No, thanks,' she had retorted curtly, not meaning it

at all. She had wanted desperately to sit down and talk, but something had held her back. 'I'll finish packing and then I'll be ready to leave.'

'Fine,' he had responded with equal coolness, surveying her with narrowed blue eyes.

With shame, Jana recalled that she had been so preoccupied with herself she had not even bothered to ask how his meeting with Ben Sinclair had gone. They had checked out of the hotel and driven out of Calgary, only speaking when absolutely necessary, until now.

She passed a tongue over her dry lips and shot a glance at Kent and, despite that turmoil inside her, couldn't stop the usual rush of pleasure that simply looking at him always gave her. Her eyes lingered over the harsh, irregular features, and with a sharp pang she reminded herself that soon there would be no more opportunities of being this close to Kent, of spending any time alone in his company. Once they were back in England, she would be out of his life completely. Maybe once in a while, she mused sadly, he might call her to salve his conscience, to ensure that she was still alive and kicking, but that would be the limit of their contact. For the first time, Jana admitted the truth to herself: it wasn't working for Kent she was going to miss—it was Kent himself. She had become used to seeing him every day, accustomed to hearing his deep, unmistakable voice greeting her every morning. She stared down at her hands and frowned. She mustn't ruin these last few days with Kent by fighting him. She swallowed, clearing her throat.

'I'd like to know about Andrew now.' She eyed him cautiously. He might have come to the end of his patience, and might refuse her request curtly, having already offered her the opportunity to talk and been coldly rebuffed. But he merely nodded resignedly. She half hoped that he might turn his head and give her a quick, sideways grin to show that he understood that she was trying to make amends, but his eyes never left the road.

She took a deep, steadying breath. 'When did you arrange it all? And why didn't you tell me before we came to Canada?' She fought that sudden flare of anger. It would achieve nothing. 'Springing it on me out of the blue like that was just such a lousy, rotten thing to do,' she murmured, trying to sound matter-of-fact.

'Andrew wanted to tell you himself,' Kent said quietly.

'And then, when it came to it, he couldn't,' Jana muttered drily, and her eyes narrowed. 'You nearly told me once, didn't you?' She recalled that moment in his office vividly. 'Why did Andrew——' she would never be able to call him Father '—suddenly want to see me after all these years?'

'I wrote to him after your mother was killed,' Kent spoke gently. 'Naturally he was very concerned about you.'

'Naturally?' Jana's voice was heavy with sarcasm. 'What? After twenty years he remembered that he had a daughter? That was kind of him.' She couldn't keep the bitterness out of her voice, forgetting her determination to remain calm and composed.

'Don't judge him when you know nothing about the circumstances,' he told her curtly.

'Of course you would side with him!' she snapped back. 'Let the woman live with the consequences.' She came to an abrupt stop. Had she no self-control at all? She was supposed to be discussing this objectively, keeping all emotion at bay. That cheap jibe at Kent had been uncalled for and unfair. She knew instinctively that he would always assume responsibility for any of his actions.

'I'm sorry,' she apologised in a small voice. 'I didn't mean that.'

He shrugged unconcernedly and she realised that she had been stupid to think that anything she could say would wound him. You had to care about someone before they could hurt you, she acknowledged. And in that moment, she recognised that the flood of bitterness and anger that had been engulfing her had nothing to do with Andrew—it had all been directed at Kent. It had been a reaction against that deep pain that had torn through her the second she had understood the reason for her presence in Canada. Her eyes darkened and she wondered why the knowledge that Kent hadn't brought her on this trip because he needed her assistance, wanted her company, should hurt quite so much. After all, hadn't she suspected right from the start that he had an ulterior motive?

Unconsciously, she chewed her bottom lip. Why didn't she stop deluding herself and admit the truth? she told herself harshly. When Kent had broken the news that she was to go to Calgary with him, it hadn't simply been the thought of seeing Canada that had filled her with such tense excitement; it had been the prospect of spending so much time alone with him.

Despite the heat of the day, Jana shivered and suddenly felt curiously vulnerable, almost naked as she sat there next to the man who was occupying her thoughts. She started to count to ten to steady herself, not trusting herself to speak until that erratic pounding of her heart had returned to normal.

Then, surprisingly, it was Kent who broke the silence, his words shocking Jana back into the present.

'Your mother had the choice,' he murmured in a low voice, 'Andrew wanted to marry her, but she refused and emigrated to England with you.'

'What?' Jana went white. All through the years of her childhood she had cherished the dream of having a secure, stable home and two parents, and that dream could have been a reality. She didn't doubt for a moment that Kent was telling her the truth, and it explained something that had been puzzling her about Andrew. He had been so far removed from the mental picture she'd always formed of her father as some irresponsible, pleasure-seeking brute of a man who had just abandoned her mother when she was pregnant. She stared up at Kent with large, confused eyes. Her mother could have married Andrew—and she had turned down his proposal. It simply didn't make sense.

'I think your mother made the right choice,' she heard Kent say. 'And don't look so shocked,' he added curtly, though Jana hadn't even been aware that he had glanced at her. Perhaps he'd just automatically guessed her reaction. 'You've met Andrew. Do you honestly think that he and your mother would have been compatible? They were totally different, worlds apart. They'd have made each other desperately unhappy.'

'How can you be so cynical?' she retorted heatedly. 'How can you tell what might have happened? Opposites attract,' she added unoriginally, but urgently wanting to believe it.

'I'm just being realistic, that's all. And so was your

mother. She had the honesty not to confuse physical infatuation with love.'

Jana absorbed the words in silence, staring out of the window but hardly registering the changing landscape, the scrubland on either side of the highway giving way to dark green pine trees as the mountains drew closer. It was surprising how little it troubled her to know that she had been the inconvenient consequence of a 'physical infatuation'. Perhaps that was because she had long ago accepted that she was the product of one of her mother's casual and frequent affairs. Her mouth curved gently. Despite everything, she had loved her mother, and still missed her intensely, haunted by the manner of her tragic death. But with cold certainty she knew that she wasn't going to live her life as had her mother. When—or if—she had a child, it would be because she wanted it desperately; it would be the result of an emotional as well as a physical union. It might be old-fashioned, but for her sex would have to be synonymous with love, the euphemism 'making love' a reality. She was convinced that anything else would just leave her with an aching emptiness.

She flicked a glance at the man by her side, and unbidden her thoughts raced back to that moment in the swimming-pool when she had felt the length of that hard, lean body against hers. With a jolt she recognised that in those few seconds she had had no control over her body's instinctive response, and suddenly nothing was clear or certain any more.

'I suppose you think your mother should have married Andrew "for the sake of the child",' Kent's sceptical voice cut through her confused thoughts. 'Surely you're not naïve enough to believe all that rubbish about children cementing relationships?' he added sardonically, and the derision in his voice made Jana flush, but it would be useless to deny that those naïve thoughts had occurred to her at one point.

'It's the stupidest of all reasons for a man and a woman to spend their life together. No one benefits and certainly not the child. I'm willing to bet that you were happier at boarding school than you would have been in a home with warring parents.'

Jana scanned the dark, averted face with wondering green eyes. There had been a rare emotion in Kent's voice and instinctively she guessed that his scathing comments had not been generalisations but had come from a more personal source.

'Your parents,' she said hesitantly, braced for a sharp snub. 'They were happy together, weren't they?'

'Sure. Until I came along,' he said flatly. There was no bitterness in his voice, no trace of self-pity, just a calm acceptance of fact. 'They weren't cut out for parenthood. A child didn't fit in with their life-style and they weren't prepared to change it.' His mouth twisted wryly. 'I didn't solve my parents' problems—I created them. One or other of them would suddenly remember my existence and accuse the other of neglecting me.' He shrugged and lapsed into silence. Jana hardly dared breathe, frightened that he would stop completely. 'As soon as I was old enough to figure out what was going on, I kept out of their way as much as possible.' His eyes were dark and reminiscent. 'I hung out at the Stewarts' most of the time.'

'That's Jake,' Jana prompted quietly.

He nodded and suddenly grinned. 'His parents

practically adopted me. I guess they didn't have
a lot of choice, seeing that I more or less lived there.'

He fell silent again and Jana stole a look at his hard,
tenacious profile, her mouth curving softly. It was
surprising how much it troubled her to think of him
as an unwanted, unloved small boy, and she felt a
warm rush of gratitude to the unknown Stewarts who
had welcomed him into their home. The thought of
Kent being completely alone as a child was somehow
unbearable.

She sat back in her seat, green eyes clouded with
thought. It was the first time he had ever talked about
his past and even then, she realised, he had given her
little more than the bare facts, injecting little emotion
into his voice. It had been left to her imagination to
picture the neglected child.

She chewed her bottom lip. Was that when Kent
had started to build up that shell of reserve,
initially as self-protection against hurt? And now,
she mused, it had become second nature for him to
depend on no one, to need no other person in his
life.

She felt strangely close to Kent in those moments,
as if she was beginning to understand the complex
man for the first time. She gazed out of the window,
not wanting to break the silence that might also break
that slim, intangible bond that had been tenuously
formed between them.

Kent halted at the toll-gate and then drove into
Banff National Park, Jana now bolt upright by his
side, turning her head from side to side, not wanting to miss anything. Everything else was
momentarily forgotten in the wonder of the awe-
inspiring mountains, their peaks still capped with
snow.

'Tell me all their names,' she pleaded and Kent, grinning at her excitement, reeled off a list of names and heights until she implored him to stop.

'Enough,' she protested. 'I'll never be able to remember half of them.'

Banff seemed to consist of one main street with avenues of bungalows and hotels branching off. Kent parked the car and Jana clambered out, sniffing the crisp air and gazing up in silent homage to the dominating, rugged mountains.

'They're just so . . .' she murmured finally, shaking her head, unable to find the right words. Did the inhabitants of this small town ever become blasé about their magnificent surroundings? Did they ever take those mountains for granted?

'Come on,' Kent smiled down at her. 'We'll eat in that restaurant across the street. They do terrific steaks.'

'I could eat a horse,' she admitted, her earlier lack of appetite seeming to have been overcome.

'Can't promise you that,' he commented drily. 'But maybe a nice piece of fresh bear meat.' He licked his lips and Jana gazed at him, horrified.

'You're kidding,' she said uncertainly as she vainly tried to match her steps to his long strides.

They had barely set foot inside the restaurant when a tall brunette clad in a smart black and white uniform came rushing to their side. Wryly, Jana wondered whether she would have received such instant attention if she had been alone, and her suspicions were confirmed as the waitress dismissed her with a brief, cursory glance and then smiled appreciatively up at Kent.

'Table for two,' he smiled back, the girl's dark beauty evidently appealing to him.

She led them to a side booth, fitted out in blue and white, and returned quickly with the menu and two glasses of iced water.

'Two steaks, please,' Kent didn't bother to consult the menu. 'One medium rare and the other,' he lifted an eyebrow in Jana's direction, 'well done.'

Her hackles rose. He hadn't even asked her what she wanted, had ordered her meal as if she were a child, incapable of making even a minor decision. The fact that she ate all her meat overcooked was irrelevant.

'Er—excuse me,' she murmured politely as the waitress moved away. 'Make that rare for me, please.' She ignored Kent's quizzical blue gaze, and watched the tall girl walk away, the waist-length, jet-black hair swinging over her shoulders.

She turned back to Kent and noticed that his attention had also been riveted to the brunette.

'She's extraordinarily beautiful,' she murmured with assumed casualness, trying to convince herself that the expression on Kent's face didn't perturb her.

'Mmm,' he agreed. 'Beautiful.'

This time she couldn't deny the way her stomach lurched at the open admiration both in his eyes and in his voice.

'Well, I'm sorry if my being here has ruined things for you,' she muttered and then could have bitten off her tongue, dreading that Kent might attribute that adolescent comment to jealousy. But to her immense relief, she saw that he was studying her with bewilderment.

'What?' he muttered and then comprehension dawned. 'Oh, I get it. You're afraid you might be cramping my style, is that it?' he said sarcastically.

'You think I'm incapable of looking at an attractive woman without automatically inviting her to my bed?'

Jana lowered her eyes, not quite sure what she had thought exactly.

'What do you think I am? Some sort of sexual athlete?'

The harshness in his voice stung her into retaliation.

'I should have thought you'd have been flattered by the description,' she commented acidly.

'What? As a boost to my fragile male ego?' he enquired, his voice deceptively soft. 'So you'd take it as a compliment if I accused you of being a nymphomaniac?'

Jana's face flooded with colour. 'Of course I wouldn't. That's not the same thing at all.' She floundered. 'I mean, it's different for you . . .'

'Really? Because I'm a man?' He raised a taunting eyebrow. 'Well, well, a liberated woman!'

Before she could think of a suitable retort, somewhat to her relief, the waitress appeared with their steaks.

'Look's good,' Kent observed and Jana deliberately averted her face, not wanting to see if he was smiling up at the waitress. Oh, lord, she suddenly cringed with burning humiliation, she was going to end up neurotic if she over-reacted like this every time Kent even looked at another woman, let alone spoke to one!

Mortified, she studied her laden plate and the sight of the blood oozing from the red lump of meat made her feel nauseous. Why on earth had she been so idiotic as to order this? What had it proved? She gritted her teeth, cut off a small piece of meat and swallowed it with her eyes closed.

'Told you they were terrific, didn't I?' Kent said with an innocence that set her teeth on edge.

'Wonderful,' she agreed brightly. She would eat every last scrap if it killed her.

Lake Louise had to be one of the most beautiful places in the world, Jana decided dreamily, looking at the snow-capped peaks reflected in the opal water below her. She watched the hikers on the opposite shore make their way up the mountain trails and wished a little wistfully that she and Kent had more time to spare. But at least she had seen the lake, she decided gratefully, gazing across from her vantage point above the boathouse to the large château at the head of the lake.

She turned her head and smiled at the sight of Kent, sprawled flat out on the grass, eyes closed. It was desperately hard not to reach out a hand and sweep back the lock of unruly black hair that had fallen across his high, proud forehead.

Her eyes softened. The tension and weariness were washed from his face; he looked younger, almost vulnerable.

He flicked open a blue eye as if aware of her scrutiny and smiled lazily. 'Guess we'd better make a move,' he murmured, sitting up.

'It's so peaceful here.' She was reluctant to leave the tranquil setting, suddenly loath to go on to Jasper to stay with Kent's friends, however nice they might be.

As he gazed across at her, his eyes dazzlingly blue, a grin softening the harsh contours of his face, she felt her heart contract. The longing just to launch herself into his arms terrified her.

Not trusting herself to speak because of that lump

in her throat, she scrambled to her feet and started to walk briskly back down the track towards the château. He caught up with her as she paused to have one last, lingering look at the view.

'Thanks for bringing me here,' she said quietly, her composure now restored.

He smiled in acknowledgement and then, catching her completely off guard, bent his head and planted a light kiss on her startled mouth.

'You look cute in that blue dress,' he said gruffly.

The kiss had been little more than a brotherly peck, the compliment hardly extravagant, but Jana was washed by furious pleasure. Kent thought she looked cute! She felt a surge of happiness as she moved on down the track by his side. Her moods seemed so transient these days; one moment she would be in the depths of despair, and then, out of the blue, she would feel as if she were standing on top of one of those incredible mountains.

They reached the car and unexpectedly Kent tossed the keys over to Jana. 'Fancy driving for a spell?'

She nodded, unable to hide her surprise. She knew the rental car had been insured in both their names, but she had just assumed that was in case of emergencies.

'You'll have to move the seat forward,' he commented as she slid into the driver's seat. 'Or you'll never reach the pedals.'

She was apprehensive at first driving with Kent beside her, convinced he was going to make some scathing, derogatory comment about her prowess, but to her surprise he remained silent and when she glanced at him she saw that he was stretched out in his seat, his eyes closed. She frowned. Had he slept at all last night?

She began to relax, getting accustomed to driving on the right as she guided the car along the deserted, paved road. Then out of the corner of her eye she saw a large, dark form amble out from the dense undergrowth. Automatically her reflexes took over and she slammed a foot on the brake.

'What the devil?' Kent's eyes shot open, his face instantly alert.

'It was a bear!' Jana's eyes glowed. 'Honestly. It just walked out right in front of the car and vanished over there.'

'What colour was it?' he suddenly barked. 'Brown? Honey?'

She frowned, puzzled. 'Black,' she said hesitantly. 'Why?'

'Aren't you going to wish, then?'

'What?' She inspected his bland face suspiciously.

'It's an old Canadian custom. If a black bear crosses your path, it's considered lucky.' He shrugged nonchalantly. 'So you wish.'

'You're pulling my leg!' she retorted swiftly, scanning his serious expression doubtfully. 'You mean like a black cat in England?' she added uncertainly.

'Exactly,' he agreed.

'I don't believe a word of it!' She started up the engine and moved off slowly. Oh, why not!

'And for heaven's sake wish with your eyes open or we'll end up in the ditch.'

She ignored him and stared straight ahead. She wished . . . oh, how she wished that Kent loved her. She ground the car to an abrupt halt.

'Not satisfied with your last emergency stop?' he enquired conversationally. 'Going to practise them all the way to Jasper?'

'You can drive now.' Was that high-pitched squeak really her voice? 'I want to look at the view,' she said, opening the car door. To her relief, Kent assented with a casual nod and they changed places quickly.

'Are you all right?' He shot her a speculative glance as he moved the car smoothly back along the road.

'Of course,' she smiled brightly. How would he react if she told him the truth, that she had committed the unpardonable sin of falling in love with him? She wondered why she should feel so shocked by the revelation, when the truth had been staring her in the face for weeks. But she had refused to admit it, avoided the issue like the plague, built up imaginary grievances against Kent, convinced herself that his attraction was purely a physical one—anything rather than face the fact that she loved him.

A well of hysteria swirled inside her. Wasn't it traditional for secretaries to become involved with their bosses? If only it were that simple, a mere passing infatuation, but, she reminded herself miserably, she had adored Kent from the moment she had first set eyes on him, the schoolgirl crush slowly changing as she grew older until it had developed into this powerful, intense emotion that threatened to engulf her completely. Her hands clenched in her lap as she stared moodily out of the window. She didn't want to love Kent! It made her too vulnerable, open to all the pain and hurt that would be the inevitable consequence of loving a man like him. But there didn't seem to be a thing she could do about it.

'Jana.'

She stiffened at the seriousness in his voice as he

spoke her name. Surely he couldn't have guessed . . .
seen something in her eyes before she had been able to
control her expression.

'That bear you saw just now might have looked cute
and cuddly, but it was a wild animal and should be
treated accordingly.'

She relaxed. 'I realise that,' she muttered tetchily.
Why did he persist in treating her as if she were an
irresponsible idiot? 'I'm not planning to feed any with
popcorn if that's what's worrying you.' In fact, she
wasn't planning to get anywhere near one.

They reached Jasper in the early evening, the small
town nestling in the valleys between the Miette and
Athabasca Rivers, hemmed in by rugged mountains
which glowed red in the setting sun.

Kent drove a short distance from the townsite and
turned up a track leading to a large campsite, the smell
of woodsmoke scenting the cool air. He drew up in
front of a neat, wooden bungalow, skirted by a
veranda.

Jana felt a burst of shyness at the prospect of
meeting his friends, though admitted that under the
circumstances it would be something of a relief not to
be alone with him any more. It would give her a
chance to come to terms with her newly accepted
feelings without the constant anxiety of his discerning
eyes upon her. Once he was with his friends, she
decided with mixed feelings, Kent wouldn't pay much
attention to her.

'Kent!'

Jana looked up quickly and saw a brown-haired girl
come hurtling out of the front door and down the
wooden steps. She flung her arms around Kent and
kissed him with a warmth he immediately

reciprocated.

Cindy Stewart looked in her late twenties, attractive rather than beautiful, with short, curly hair and warm, hazel eyes. Her stocky figure was clad casually in faded jeans and a checked shirt several sizes too large for her.

Jana felt a twinge of envy at the ease with which the other girl stood with her arm crooked through Kent's. Before the latter had the chance to start the introductions, a giant of a man with shaggy, dark hair came pounding across the site towards them.

'Kent, old buddy!' He slapped his friend on the back with a force, Jana thought with quiet amusement, that would have sent most men flying.

'Jake, Cindy, this is Jana Morton, my secretary.'

'Pleased to meet you, Jana.' Cindy smiled warmly and extended a hand.

'Thank you.' Jana smiled shyly, taking hold of the proffered hand.

'Come on in.' Cindy moved up the steps. 'Those two great hulking brutes can bring in the luggage.' She grinned, her eyes scanning the two men affectionately. 'And they accuse us women of gossiping!'

Jana laughed, instantly drawn to the cheerful, good-natured young woman, and then she froze as Jake's voice drifted up to her, his words quite distinct in the still, evening air.

'Not bad, old buddy, not bad at all. Secretary's a bit unoriginal, though.' He guffawed insinuatingly. 'Not your usual type, either.'

Jana didn't hesitate. She jumped down the steps and stormed across to the huge man.

'For your information, I am not Kent's . . .

anything.' She confronted him furiously. 'And I hate crude, snide innuendoes!' Her eyes blazed with angry, green fire.

There was a moment's stunned silence, enough time for her to see the stony, ice-cold glint in Kent's eyes. He would never forgive her for this, she thought frantically.

Then, abruptly, the giant in front of her let out a mighty bellow of laughter, and from behind Jana was surprised to hear a murmur of approval from Cindy.

'Good for you, Jana.' The stocky girl walked across to her husband, the love in her soft eyes belying her pretended severity. 'That'll teach you to open your big mouth before you think!'

Jake Stewart started to shake with laughter again and then, wiping his eyes with a massive, callused hand, he grinned down at the slim figure in front of him.

'I think, Jana Morton, that you and me are going to get along real fine.' He winked. 'And maybe you're not Kent's type—but you're certainly mine.'

'Hey, you cut that out,' Cindy mocked him, grinning widely at Jana. 'And get back to work—there's a camper just driven in!'

Jake moved away to deal with the trailer, accompanied by Kent, the latter's swift, lithe movements contrasting oddly with the rolling, ambling gait of the heavier man.

Jana followed Cindy into the house, the other girl eagerly firing questions at her about England which, beginning to wish she had read a tourist guide of her own country before leaving, Jana did her best to answer.

'Want a glass of lemonade?' Cindy invited as they entered a room overlooking the campsite. 'Or would you like to freshen up first?'

Jana opted for the drink and sat down on a shabby but comfortable chair, surveying the untidy room with its unpretentious furnishings with pleasure. This was a room that people actually lived in, she decided approvingly.

'Bit of a mess, isn't it,' her hostess commented cheerfully as she returned with two glasses. 'Jake has to be the most untidy man on this earth, and,' she admitted happily, 'I guess I'm not much better.' She pushed aside a pile of old magazines and sat down on the sofa.

'This is lovely,' Jana smiled as she took a sip of the home-made lemonade, feeling comfortable and at ease in the older girl's company. 'How long have you and Jake been running the campsite?'

'About eight years now,' Cindy answered promptly. 'It's kind of fun meeting loads of different people. I really like it here and it's great for Jake. He'd hate working in an office.'

Jana nodded understandingly, unable to imagine the huge man cooped up inside four walls for very long.

'Of course he still hankers after the circuit.' Cindy grimaced and then grinned. 'But I told him that if he ever went back to it, I'd walk out.' She sighed. 'Not that I really would, of course.'

'What's the circuit?'

'Rodeo,' Cindy explained succinctly. 'Jake and Kent used to play cowboys.' There was an underlying seriousness in the seemingly flippant, derisory remark. 'Bronc-busting, steer-wrestling, bull-riding—they did the lot. Jake needed the money for high school and college.' She shrugged. 'I never did quite figure out why Kent got involved.' There was no envy in her voice for the evident fact that Kent's parents had been financially better off than Jake's. 'I guess it was for the excitement. And the challenge.'

'Yes,' Jana nodded wryly. She could well understand what had motivated Kent.

The other girl heaved a sigh. 'I used to be scared to death,' she confessed. 'Lord knows why men have to do these crazy things.' She shrugged. 'They were both pretty experienced and never took chances, but it was just so damn dangerous. And Jake expected me to go along and cheer!' She laughed. 'Which of course I did. I reckon love makes you soft in the head.'

Jana lowered her eyes quickly and said casually, 'But you persuaded Jake to give it up in the end?' It was Kent she wanted to hear about, she acknowledged ruefully, but she was wary of asking any direct questions about him.

Cindy was quiet for a moment, a troubled expression creeping over her placid face, and Jana wondered apprehensively if she had inadvertently made a gaffe. She hadn't intended to pry into the Stewarts' personal relationship.

'Everything changed after Chris died,' Cindy said quietly, shaking her head slowly. 'Something just seemed to get into Kent. He wasn't careful any more, he took risks, became really reckless.' She paused, face sombre. 'It was as if he didn't care what happened to him any more, as if he wanted to kill himself. It was real scary to watch him.' She gave a small smile. 'And of course Jake had to try and keep up with him.'

'What happened?' Jana asked quietly.

Cindy shrugged resignedly. 'Jake got busted up pretty badly.'

'Oh, how awful.' Jana's eyes widened with sympathy, only too easily imagining what the other girl must have suffered at the time.

'Well, at least that seemed to make Kent come to his senses before he broke his neck. He waited until Jake came out of hospital and then just announced that he was quitting Canada and going to England.'

Jana frowned, still puzzled. 'You'd have thought that if this Chris was killed at the rodeo, it would have made Kent more careful.' She was appalled not just by the tragedy of the unknown man, but at the terrible knowledge that the same fate could have befallen Kent. Suddenly, she was conscious that Cindy was staring at her with startled eyes.

'Chris . . . Chrissie . . . wasn't one of the rodeo guys. I thought you knew. She was Jake's sister.' Before Jana had time to register the words, she jumped to her feet and took down one of the many photographs that adorned the mantelpiece of the open fireplace.

'Here,' she handed it to Jana. 'That's Chrissie.'

Hesitantly, Jana stared down at the coloured snapshot, numbly taking in a young, less severe-looking Kent, clad in a dark suit, his head bent down towards a young, brown-haired girl in a yellow dress. They weren't touching; they had no need. The unspoken allegiance in their eyes as they gazed at each other was captured for all time.

'It was taken at our wedding. Kent was best man and Chrissie was my chief bridesmaid. It's the last photo we have of her.'

'She was lovely,' Jana said simply.

'Mmm; I still miss her like crazy even after all this time.' Cindy's voice trembled. 'I guess we all do.'

'Kent carries her photo in his wallet,' Jana said quietly and the Canadian girl nodded understandingly.

'I don't think he's ever really got over it. Of course it helped Jake that he could talk about it, get it all out of his system. But Kent——' she sighed '—he just keeps everything closed up inside of him.'

Jana knew only too well. 'How did Chrissie die?' she asked gently after a few moments, and then, as Cindy's eyes darkened with pain, regretted the question. She didn't want to open old wounds.

'She took an overdose.'

'What?' Jana gasped incredulously, and vividly she recalled Kent's over-reaction when he had discovered her taking the sleeping tablets, everything now clear.

Before she had time to recollect herself, there was a knock on the outer door and Cindy stood up with a wry smile.

'That's the chief drawback of this job. You're on call twenty-four hours a day.' She moved across the room. 'Won't be long. Help yourself to another drink from the fridge if you want.' She grimaced. 'Sorry my conversation hasn't exactly been cheerful. Jake always says I talk too much!' Her eyes rested on the younger girl thoughtfully. 'You're a pretty good listener, though.'

Jana smiled vaguely as Cindy left the room. However good a listener she might be, she mused sadly, there was one person who would never confide in her.

She stared down at the patterned carpet, still shocked by Cindy's revelation. Why had that beautiful girl taken her own life? It seemed so incomprehensible, such an appalling waste. That girl had had everything to live for—she had been loved by Kent.

CHAPTER FIVE

JANA lay on her stomach, chin cupped in her hands, gazing into the flickering flames of the campfire. She knew without looking round that Kent sat a few feet behind her, long legs stretched out, his back resting against the stout trestle table on which they had eaten supper.

'Stick another log on, Jana,' Jake murmured lazily. 'You're nearest.'

He sat close to Cindy, his arm resting casually across her shoulder with an easy familiarity that Jana tried hard not to envy.

She stood up, brushed the knees of her jeans and moved across to the wood-pile. The campsite was dotted with the glow of fires, the scent of woodsmoke mingling in the crisp, night air with the more pungent aroma of barbecued food.

Someone in the darkness began to pick out a soft, plaintive tune on a guitar, and for a moment, Jana stood motionless, lost in a web of enchantment. Then automatically her eyes were drawn to the lean, craggy face, the glow of the fire casting mysterious shadows over the hard planes, and her heart lurched. Controlling a wistful sigh, she picked up a piece of wood and tossed it on to the fire, sending amber sparks shooting up into the starry, velvet sky.

'Have you two made any plans for tomorrow?' asked Cindy idly, lifting her head from her husband's shoulder. Seeing Jana's uncertain expression, she grinned. 'Hey, Kent, why don't you take Jana up Whistler's Mountain for the day?'

'Where's that?' asked Jana immediately, eyes lighting with interest.

'Couple of miles south of the townsite,' Cindy told her. 'The mountain's called after the whistling marmots—you can see them up there if you're lucky, though you're more likely to see squirrels.' She paused. 'There's a sky tram that takes you to the top and the view from there is fantastic.'

Jana grinned, catching the other girl's enthusiasm, her love and pride for her native country only too evident. 'Sounds wonderful,' she commented, looking across at Kent warily, trying to gauge his mood, but his expression was concealed by the creeping shadows.

'Tell you what,' he drawled. 'Why don't you take Jana tomorrow, Cindy, and I'll stay here and help Jake with the chores.'

There was a moment's silence in which Jana was conscious of both the Stewarts' eyes upon her, and she felt as if she were the prize for the person who drew the shortest straw. First prize, one day out with Jana; second prize, two days out with Jana.

Then Cindy broke in warmly. 'Sure. It'll be great to have female company for a change.'

Jake intervened with a broad grin. 'Not like you, buddy, to prefer my company to that of a pretty girl.' He winked at Jana. 'I've an even better idea. How about Cindy staying here with you, and I'll take Jana.'

She threw him a grateful smile, but nothing could salve that hurt that Kent had publicly shown himself so unwilling to spend any more time with her that was absolutely necessary. She frowned. What on earth was the matter with her? She was being far too sensitive. It was perfectly natural that Kent should want to spend the day with one of his oldest friends in preference to her.

Everyone lapsed into somnolent silence, broken eventually by Cindy who rose lethargically to her feet.

'One thing about eating outdoors, there's not too many dishes to do.' She started to collect the empty plates, Jana immediately assisting her.

'That was delicious,' she said, following Cindy into the kitchen.

'Thank Kent, he was the one who cooked it,' the Canadian girl smiled back, running hot water into a bowl.

Jana nodded, remembering how relaxed and carefree he had looked as he tended the lamb chops over the fire, responding to Jake's bantering with his innate dry humour.

'Actually, I'm kind of glad to have you on my own for a minute,' Cindy suddenly confessed with a slightly embarrassed frown. 'When Kent called us up this morning and said he was bringing a girl along, Jake and I just assumed . . . well, we've only the one spare room.'

Jana understood straight away; the Stewarts had taken it for granted that Kent would be sleeping with the woman he had brought with him.

'But I guess you and Kent don't have that kind of relationship,' Cindy said hesitantly, her eyes revealing her curiosity. 'So if you want, I'll put up a camp-bed for you some place. That's one thing we have plenty of round here!'

Jana tried to look nonchalant. It wasn't difficult to

understand how Cindy had come to the conclusion that she and Kent were not lovers. His manner towards her that evening had hardly been loverlike; he had sat several feet away from her, giving her little more than the odd cursory glance.

'Our relationship is through marriage,' Jana said wryly, and explained briefly, seeing the growing surprise on the older girl's face.

'Honestly, Kent really does carry the strong, dark, silent type to the extreme,' she exclaimed, and Jana couldn't stop a bubble of laughter welling up inside of her. 'You'd think he'd have told us you were his stepsister, instead of letting Jake and me think . . .' She raised exasperated eyes upwards. 'I mean, we knew his father had remarried, but Kent never said a word about you.'

Jana shrugged carelessly, trying to ignore the stab of pain. 'I suppose it slipped his mind.' She was appalled at the bitterness in her voice, conscious of Cindy's sudden searing scrutiny.

'You love him, don't you?' Her voice was gentle but matter-of-fact.

Jana's face was suffused with warm colour. 'I . . . er . . .' she stammered. 'I don't know,' she finally said dully. She turned bewildered eyes to Cindy's kind face. 'It's nothing like I ever imagined it would be . . .' She had expected love to come slowly when it came, expected it to feel as if she were being enveloped in a warm, secure cocoon. Nothing had prepared her for this perpetual, nagging ache, those moments of explosion inside her. But then, Jana reminded herself miserably, she had always assumed that she would be loved in return. She bit her lip.

'Does it show?' she asked, cramped with panic that if Cindy had guessed so easily, Kent must surely know too. And then he would never go anywhere near her again; he would never forgive her for becoming emotionally involved with him.

'Hey,' the other girl said softly. 'Don't look so terrified. I'm not going to tell Kent.'

'No.' To her horror, the tears started to pour down Jana's cheek. 'I'm sorry, I don't know what's the matter.'

Cindy put her arms around her, comforting her until her sobbing eased. 'Men,' she muttered disgustedly. 'Why do we bother?'

'I'm all right now.' Jana gave a wan smile, and then something that had been puzzling her came back into her mind. 'Did you say Kent only told you this morning that he'd be bringing me along too?'

'Yes. But don't worry about that. I'm always glad of female company. And pretty glad it turned out to be someone like you,' she grinned. 'And not one of those glamour girls he always seems to have in tow.' A hand flew to her mouth. 'Pretty tactful, aren't I?'

She looked so crestfallen that Jana couldn't help grinning at her. 'You mean I don't strike you as the sophisticated type?' she teased, picking up a tea-towel.

Jake and Kent were talking desultorily when the two girls emerged from the bungalow. Seeing his wife approach, Jake stood up.

'Better do the last round.'

'I'll come with you, honey,' Cindy said immediately, and Jana tensed, hoping that this wasn't the other girl's idea of being tactful, because right then the last person she wanted to be alone with was Kent.

She sat down silently, as far away from him as possible.

'You all right?' he asked abruptly, and Jana averted her face, dreading that those all-too-observant blue eyes would see tear-stains on her cheeks, even though she had dabbed at her face with cold water before leaving the kitchen.

'Of course I am,' she said sharply. 'Why shouldn't I be?' She saw his face tighten and bit her lip. Kent had asked her a civilised question and she had snapped his head off.

He shrugged. 'Just not like you to be so quiet,' he said idly.

'You didn't expect me to be coming with you to Jasper, did you?' She blurted out what had been nagging in her mind, asking him the question she had forbidden herself to ask.

'What?' he demanded, perplexed.

'Cindy said you only phoned this morning to say I'd be coming as well,' she explained, forcing herself to sound light.

'I see.'

'Is that all you can say? I see?' she flared, control snapping. 'Why can't you be honest with me? You thought that Andrew would ask me to stay with him, didn't you?' What a fool she had been. It was so obvious now that Kent had never intended her to share this short holiday with him. He had brought her to Canada, probably planning to hand her over to Andrew as if she were a piece of lost luggage soon after they arrived. 'So what went wrong? Andrew have an unexpected business trip?' Appalled, she came to an abrupt halt. She must be out of her mind; she was sounding like a self-pitying, nagging wife in some kitchen-sink drama.

'What the hell's got into you?' Kent thundered. 'Aren't you enjoying yourself?'

'Of course I am,' she squeaked, wishing that she could just climb into a hole and bury herself.

'Then in heaven's name, why do you have to start ranting and raving like a lunatic about nothing?' His voice was like ice. 'I've come here to see some old friends, to relax—not to pamper to you in a paddy!' He jumped to his feet and stormed off into the darkness, leaving Jana sitting in stupefied silence, awash with shame and embarrassment, wishing desperately that the last few moments had never happened.

The view from the top of Whistler's Mountain was as spectacular as Jana had been promised, but it was Cindy by her side as they strolled through the alpine tundra, Cindy who pointed out the snow-capped peak of Mount Robson, Cindy who shared the breathtaking view of the Athabasca and Miette river valleys from the sky-deck balcony—and it should have been Kent. And somehow, as much as she liked the other girl, and even though it was an experience she would never forget, the whole day was marred for Jana because Kent wasn't there to share it with her.

With horror, she wondered if she was going to spend the rest of her life like this, never enjoying anything to the full because Kent wasn't by her side. Where on earth was her pride, her independence?

If Jana was unnaturally bright and vivacious over the next few days, Kent made no comment; either because he hadn't noticed or because he just wasn't interested, she decided miserably, gazing up at the ceiling from her camp-bed on Thursday morning.

Sighing, she glanced at her watch. Five o'clock. Jake and Cindy wouldn't stir for at least another half-hour, but she couldn't go back to sleep, even though she was convinced she had lain awake all night, tossing and turning.

She threw back the sheet and padded over to the window, drawing back the curtains. The clear azure sky and sparkling, dew-touched grass lifted her spirits, and sent out an invitation it was impossible to ignore. Swiftly, she turned away from the window and tugged on her jeans and green sweater. She wouldn't be long; she'd just go for a meander around the campsite, and be back before anyone missed her.

The campsite was still and deserted; it was if she were the only person on the planet. Lost in thought, Jana strolled around the perimeter of the site, and absently started up a track on the far side. Today, she and Kent were heading back to Calgary, stopping off on the way to see Andrew Jameson. She frowned apprehensively and sat down on a log, eyes staring unseeingly at the ground.

Half of her wished that Andrew had never been introduced into her life, the other half was curious. But, she acknowledged wryly, she couldn't just automatically love a stranger because he was her biological father. She sighed. If only Kent had prepared her for this. Her eyes glazed over and then she roused herself irritably. She had come out here to think about her father, not Kent. Why did her thoughts always come back to the dark-haired man?

She jerked her head up, conscious of the rustling sound coming from the surrounding undergrowth, uncertain of how long it had been going on. Probably a rabbit, or even a deer, she reassured herself. Still, it was about time she started back. In her dreamy state she had walked further than she had intended. She rose to her feet and began to head back down the track, then her body froze with an icy shudder and her mouth went dry as a large brown shape materialised in front of her.

Don't make any sudden, jerky movement, she told herself, amazed at how clear her mind was, almost detached, as the adrenalin coursed round her body. Desperately she tried to recall everything she had read in that leaflet Kent had insisted she study, and then she couldn't stop the muffled gasp of terror as the bear rose to its hind legs, its head swinging from side to side as it tried to focus its weak eyes. It was useless to run, useless to climb a tree. Bears could run as fast as racehorses and were agile climbers.

'Don't move, Jana. Just keep calm.' She heard Kent's voice, quiet and soothing, and for a moment she wondered if she was going crazy and had imagined it in her terror. Then, out of the corner of her eye, she saw the shadowy figure and then sensed his presence behind her.

Jana felt as if her heart had stopped beating as the bear fell to all fours and began to approach.

'Play dead.' Kent's voice was urgent in her ear. 'Lie down on your front and curl up.'

She didn't hesitate. Her trust in him was absolute. She slumped to the ground, lifted her knees up to her chest and clasped her hands over the back of her head. Clearly she recalled the instructions in the leaflet about 'playing dead' as a last resort, and knew that, without Kent, she would never have had the courage to do so. In the end, she acknowledged with cold certainty, she would have tried to run.

Then she felt Kent's weight on top of her and her sick terror was all for him, lying there exposed as he protected her with his own body. It was all her fault . . . he was going to be maimed or worse, and it was all because of her.

How long they lay there, Jana had no idea. It seemed like eternity. And then she felt Kent's weight being lifted from her and she was being pulled roughly to her feet.

For one long second, Jana remained immobile, eyes huge with shock in her ashen face; then she flung her arms around Kent's neck, clutching at him desperately. She felt sick with the awful knowledge of what might have been, of the terrible injuries that could have been inflicted on Kent as he shielded her. She ached to feel his arms around her, hear his voice, calm, soothing—and alive. But his arms remained stiffly by his side, and self-consciously she eased herself away from him, scanning his furious face with dark, apprehensive eyes.

'What the hell did you think you were playing at, wandering out here on your own?' His voice cut through her like a razor.

'I thought it would be safe . ... near the campsite.' A blazing row with Kent was something she couldn't cope with right now.

'Haven't you any common sense? Didn't it occur to you that a campsite spells out food to a hungry bear?' Narrowed, ice-blue eyes raked her flushed face.

'I'm sorry,' she mumbled defeatedly, remembering now, too late, how Jake had lamented the fact that, despite all his warnings, campers still left food and rubbish lying around in the open. 'How did you find me?' she added weakly.

He didn't answer, and before she had time to register what was happening he had reached out an arm and pulled her roughly against him, his mouth covering hers in a brutal, savage kiss that was as punishing as a physical blow.

He raised his head and she looked up at him with

glazed eyes, her mouth sore and bruised.

'Come on,' he ordered brusquely. 'I'll have to borrow one of Jake's hunting rifles.'

'You're going to sh-shoot the bear?' she gasped in horror.

'Wouldn't you like a nice bear-rug for your hearth?' he rasped and then, as he saw the disgust in her eyes, he relented. 'I'm only going to frighten it away from the area,' his mouth tightened, 'in case someone else decides this is Regent's Park and takes an early-morning stroll.' He turned on his heel and strode back towards the site, Jana, crimson with humiliation, hurrying by his side.

Kent hadn't spoken to her for the last half-hour, she realised with aching misery, feeling lonelier than she would have ever thought possible, sitting there beside him in the car.

Jana controlled her despairing sigh, a wry smile on her face as she remembered the affectionate farewell the Stewarts had bestowed upon her, extending an open invitation for her to return at any time. There had been Cindy's last, knowing grin and her whispered 'Good luck', and Jana had known that the wishes weren't just for the ordeal ahead with her father.

But luck wouldn't help the situation with Kent; nothing would. Her tongue explored her bruised mouth tentatively and without pleasure. That kiss hadn't been prompted out of passion or desire, but brutally executed out of fury. Her relationship with Kent seemed to be deteriorating by the hour; the proximity of the last few days, instead of bringing them closer, had merely increased that chasm between them. He had been relaxed and cheerful in the

Stewarts' company, but on the rare occasions he had been left alone with her he had treated her with cool indifference, his conversation little more than curt monosyllables, while she, unnerved and self-conscious, had chattered non-stop.

Downcast, she stared out of the window, realising that Kent had turned off the highway and they were now travelling up a narrow road, edged by thick pine trees.

'Where are we?' she asked as the road petered out to little more than a dirt-track. 'In the middle of nowhere?'

'Believe it or not, only about thirty miles from Calgary.'

At least he was talking to her again, Jana consoled herself as they passed under a wooden sign that announced that they were now on the Flying J.

'How big is the ranch?' she asked curiously.

'About three thousand acres.'

'Heavens!' She couldn't visualise that much land but it sounded enormous. 'Does Andrew work it himself?'

Kent shook his head. 'He has a foreman.' He was silent for a moment and then added unexpectedly, 'Jake and I used to come over and help out in our vacations.'

'When you weren't rodeo-riding?' Jana said unthinkingly, and saw his eyes narrow. 'Cindy told me,' she added hesitantly.

'I see. And what else did she tell you?' There was an edge to his voice.

'Nothing much,' she assured him, not daring to reveal the extent of their conversation. 'We'd more interesting things to talk about than you!'

The trees abruptly gave way to pasture and ahead

lay a huge farmhouse, set between barns and stables. Jana went cold.

'Kent,' she turned to him urgently. 'I can't go through with this. Turn round. Please.'

'What? But you've already met Andrew.'

'That was different. I didn't know who he was then.' Her voice wavered as Kent drew up in front of the house. 'Do I look all right?' She wished now that she had worn a dress instead of her jeans and green T-shirt. Frantically, she delved into her handbag for a comb and lipstick.

'Jana.' Kent's hand suddenly covered hers. 'You look——' he gave an odd, enigmatic smile '—you look just fine.'

She hardly heard him, didn't have time to analyse the curious expression in his eyes, her whole attention was strained to the man coming down the steps to greet them. He looked as nervous and awkward as she felt and that somehow boosted her confidence.

He didn't attempt to hug or kiss her, merely said with his shy, lopsided smile, 'I'm glad you've come.'

'Yes, so am I,' she responded immediately, and found that the words were sincere.

'Right, I'll see you later,' Kent murmured and Jana threw him a startled glance. He couldn't be thinking of leaving her in her hour of need.

'Won't you stay for lunch?' Andrew asked quickly, but Kent refused courteously.

'I'll pick you up this evening,' he told Jana, but Andrew intervened quickly.

'Oh, I can run Jana back to Calgary.'

The two men shook hands, and as Kent strode back to the car Jana sped after him, under the pretext of having left something inside it.

'Kent,' she implored in a hoarse whisper. 'You can't leave me here on my own. Please stay.'

His eyes met hers. 'Andrew wants to see you, not me,' he said quietly. 'You need time alone together.'

'But Kent . . .' she pleaded.

'I'll see you back at the hotel,' he cut across her protest and the engine roared into life.

It was the strangest few hours of Jana's young life. At first father and daughter were wary of each other, and then slowly they both relaxed, and Andrew began to talk in his soft, slow drawl, answering the hundreds of questions Jana put to him with a frankness and honesty that drew her to him. She understood in those hours how much he had loved her mother.

'You've never married?' she quizzed him gently, and he shook his head.

'Oh, there have been women, of course.' He paused. 'But your mother was the only one I ever wanted to share my life with.'

Jana was appalled by the pathos. How awful to spend your whole life wanting just one person, and never to have them.

'I wanted to come and see you, many, many times,' Andrew confessed to his daughter. 'But I thought it best to stay out of your life completely.' He smiled. 'Your mother wrote to me from time to time. Sent me photos of you.'

Jana was unable to stop the glisten of tears in her eyes, and then, with sudden certainty, knew the answer to her next question. 'You paid my school fees, didn't you?'

He nodded silently.

Andrew drove her back to Calgary that evening, and

as they shared an easy, companionable silence, Jana knew that, given time, she could easily grow to love the shy, unassuming man who was her father.

He dropped her outside the hotel.

'You'll let me know what you decide, then?'

'Yes,' she nodded, grateful that he wasn't pressing her for an immediate answer to the question he had put to her just as they were leaving the ranch. She knew, too, that whatever reply she finally gave him he would accept, that he wouldn't exert any emotional pressure on her to change her mind. Impulsively Jana leant over and gave him a light kiss on the cheek, the pleasure in his eyes rewarding her more than any words could have done.

She went up to the reception desk to check in, and with wry amusement discovered that Kent had somehow managed to obtain two separate rooms this time. The receptionist produced her key and then told her with a smile, 'Mr Tyson left a message for you. He's in the bar.'

'Thanks,' said Jana, and turned away indecisively. Should she go and change first? No, she needed desperately to talk to Kent; more than that, she admitted with a lurch of her stomach, after only seven hours away from him, she ached to see him.

She spotted him immediately, sitting in a corner with his back to the door, and then with a droop of her spirits she registered that he wasn't alone. Next to him was a tall, tawny-haired girl. Rowena Fenner, the Freedom girl, whose face would soon be plastered all over the billboards, whose perfect figure would be seen on television and in countless magazines advertising the new range of casual and sporting wear. She was ideal for the part, Jana was forced to admit, with her fresh, glowing face: the perfect beautiful, active, outdoor girl.

Abruptly, Jana turned away, but it was too late, Rowena had seen her and was waving, Kent now turning his head, too.

'Hi, Jana.' Rowena gave her a wide smile, looking cool and elegant in a simple midnight-blue dress that showed off her thick, rich hair to perfection, making Jana even more conscious of her dishevelled appearance in dusty jeans and T-shirt. And she probably smelt of horse too, she thought ruefully, recalling Andrew's conducted tour of the stables.

'Hello, Rowena,' Jana smiled back. 'When did you arrive?'

'A couple of hours ago.' Rowena rose to her feet in a slow, graceful movement. 'I was just leaving.' She grimaced. 'If I don't get an early night, there's no way I'm going to look the epitome of healthy, clean living in the morning!' She grinned and bent her head towards Kent, brushing his mouth lightly with her lips. 'See you tomorrow.'

Jana tried to quell that tingle in her veins, tried to ignore the way Kent's eyes followed Rowena across the room. What made it worse, she realised gloomily, was that not only was Rowena stunningly attractive, she had a personality to match.

'What would you like to drink?' Kent enquired.

'Orange, please.' She sat down on the stool vacated by Rowena, noticing that as usual Kent was receiving instant attention from the waiter.

'How did it go?' he asked quietly as her drink appeared in seconds.

'Fine,' she answered lightly, and then, unable to keep it back any longer, she blurted out, 'Andrew's asked me to go and live with him.' Her eyes raked his face, eager to see his reaction, but to her surprise his expression didn't alter. 'You guessed that he'd ask me, didn't you?' she asked slowly.

'It seemed likely,' he admitted. 'Come on, Jana, it can't have come as a complete shock to you.'

'It did,' she said quietly, and saw him raise a sceptical eyebrow but decided to ignore it.

'And what have you decided to do?'

Jana stiffened with stunned hurt. His voice was as coolly polite as if he were asking her to select something from a dinner menu, making it quite evident that it was a matter of complete indifference to him what she did.

'I haven't made up my mind yet,' she said carefully. 'It's a pretty big decision.'

'Is it?' he said carelessly. 'I should have thought you'd have jumped at the chance.' He tossed back the whisky he had been nursing in his hand. 'Face it—what is there back in England for you? No family, no job, a dingy rented flat.' He shrugged. 'What do you have to lose? If things don't work out with Andrew, you can always go back to England and you're no worse off.'

Quickly Jana swallowed her orange juice, not wanting to hear any more, and pushed back her stool noisily. 'I'm going to bed. Goodnight, Kent,' she muttered gruffly and rushed away, suddenly desperate to reach the sanctity of her hotel room.

Mechanically she prepared for bed, and then stood for a long time in the darkened room, staring out of the window at the city lights beyond.

Andrew was offering her the chance of a new life, a luxurious home, financial security. And, more important than any of those things, he was her father, her only living relative. Kent was right, she admitted dully: most girls would jump at the opportunity being given to them. There really was nothing to entice her back to London. Her throat was constricted. Except for the most important thing in the world—Kent.

Her eyes darkened moodily. The most difficult decision of her life—and it all hinged on Kent. If she remained in Canada when he flew back to London, she might never see him again . . . Surely anything would be better than that? She could put up with her shabby flat, a tedious job—just as long as there was the hope of seeing Kent occasionally. The thought of being separated from him by thousands of miles was too dreadful even to contemplate. After all, she could always come out to see Andrew for holidays.

Slowly, she moved across the room and sat down on her bed. Anyway, she didn't have to make up her mind just yet; in fact, she supposed there was no reason why she couldn't return to England with Kent, and fly back at a later date if she chose. So there was no point in lying awake all night brooding, she admonished herself firmly, drawing back the sheet and climbing into bed. But as she closed her eyes she knew that she had already reached her decision.

She was seldom alone with Kent over the next few days, following him around like a dutiful shadow as they attended store promotions, fashion shows, business meetings and lunches, and the hectic schedule gave her little time to think about anything but the matter in hand.

It was impossible, too, not to be affected by the enthusiastic jubilation that swept Calgary with the start of the Stampede, the entertainment not confined to Stampede Park but overflowing into the city centre, with its street dancers and musicians, mini parades, free pancake breakfasts.

To bill the Calgary Exhibition and Stampede as the greatest outdoor show on earth was no exaggeration, Jana decided, shielding her eyes against the glare of the early-afternoon sun as she stood watching Rowena, perched up on a chuckwagon, assume various poses as instructed by the briskly efficient young photographer. Stampede Park was the perfect location for publicity shots of the Freedom girl, with the exciting and colourful backdrop of the rodeo, the authentic Indian encampment, the re-created Wild West town.

Jana had been astounded by the size of the Stampede grounds when she first saw them. She had expected the huge outdoor stadium in which the rodeo events and evening chuckwagon races took place, but she hadn't been expecting the enormous livestock show, the numerous fascinating exhibitions, the live stage-entertainments, the sideshows. Added to all that, there was a gigantic funfair. It would take all of the ten days the show lasted to see everything, Jana realised.

'Enjoying your first Stampede?'

She had known before he spoke that Kent had come up behind her, seeming to have developed an extra sense where he was concerned.

'I'm loving it,' she responded, flicking him a glance. He stood by her side, arms folded across his powerful chest, eyes narrowed against the sun, clad in Levis and a blue shirt, looking as rugged and tough as any of the cowboys she had seen.

He was watching Rowena, but his assessment of the tawny-haired girl was purely professional. For the moment she wasn't a stunningly attractive girl, merely an employee doing her job.

'Pity you won't get a chance to see the chuckwagon races this evening,' Kent remarked casually, his attention never wavering from the photographer and his subject. Except for this final outdoor photographic session, the campaign was over and Ben Sinclair was hosting a party that night to celebrate its success. A party to which Jana wasn't much looking forward.

'Still, I guess there will be other years,' he added idly.

The implication of his words struck Jana immediately—the casual assumption that she would be living in Canada next year. She tried to ignore the stab of pain that tore into her as she realised just how easily Kent was able to dismiss her from his life.

Rowena climbed down elegantly from the wagon amid a barrage of ribald but good-natured comments from the crowd of onlookers, and made her way to the small trailer to change her outfit, followed by her retinue of assistants.

'Is it OK if I go and have a wander around for a while?' Jana enquired restlessly. 'I seem to be superfluous to requirements at the moment.' All she had done so far that day was to supply the young photographer with hot dogs and Cokes.

Kent suddenly grinned down at her and, as she encountered the dazzling blue eyes, Jana's heart flipped over. Oh, lord, she thought despairingly. Please don't smile at me like that! She could control her betraying thoughts when he treated her with his habitual cool, casual indifference, but when, out of the blue, he smiled at her like this, her defences were torn to shreds.

'I think we're both superfluous right now,' he mocked her. 'They should be winding up pretty soon anyway.' He glanced at his wristwatch. 'Come on.'

Before Jana had time to grasp what was happening, she was being propelled through the crowd.

'Where are we going?' she asked weakly.

'I've a couple of tickets for this afternoon's rodeo.' He quirked a teasing dark eyebrow at her startled face. 'Hey, you can't come to Stampede and not see at least one bucking bronc!'

The bareback riding had started when they slipped into their seats and Jana watched the horses bucking and careering around the stadium with mounting apprehension, wondering how on earth the riders managed to stay on for even one second.

'Why do they keep one arm up in the air?' she demanded of Kent. Surely it would make more sense to clutch those fearsome horses with both arms?

'They'll be disqualified if they touch the horse with both hands,' Kent explained. 'They hold their free hand in the air so the judge can see. It helps them keep their balance, too.'

She shuddered as the less successful riders hit the ground with alarming frequency, secretly astounded that they weren't injured but scrambled to their feet, unconcernedly raising their hats to the cheering crowds.

The next event was bull-riding, and Jana watched with fascinated horror as cowboys thundered into the arena astride the twisting, spinning, ferocious-looking animals. Those who weren't tossed to the ground but managed to remain seated until the klaxon went still had to dismount avoiding the pounding hooves and savage horns. Jana quickly grasped that the clowns that kept appearing weren't merely to entertain the crowd but had the more serious function of trying to divert the bulls' attention as the riders clambered to safety.

Then, as one rider was tossed from the bull and
landed right under the stamping hooves, Jana
flinched, averting her face, unconsciously clutching
hold of Kent's arm.

'Hey, it's all right,' he reassured her. 'Look. He's
safe behind the barrier.'

She breathed a sigh of relief, self-consciously taking
her hand from his arm, but she still felt sick. That
man in the stadium could have been pounded
senseless by those hooves—or worse. A new wave of
nausea engulfed her. Once, that man in the ring could
have been Kent! She glanced up at him, wondering
what he was thinking—whether he was reliving old
memories, perhaps even hankering after his old life.
She forced her attention back to the stadium, but
wasn't altogether sorry when Kent announced that it
was time they left.

'Would you like a cold drink?' he asked, guiding her
through the stadium, his height and breadth making
an instant pathway for them as they merged with the
crowds outside.

'Yes, please,' she answered gratefully, realising
how hot, thirsty and sticky she felt with the afternoon
sun beating down on her unprotected head. She was
beginning to appreciate why so many of the native
Calgarians wore those wide-brimmed cowboy hats.

They paused by a kiosk and Kent delved into the
pocket of his jeans for a handful of coins. He
examined them briefly and then tossed one over to
Jana. 'Picked this up for you this morning when I
went to the bank,' he murmured casually.

Jana stared down at the silver Calgary Stampede
souvenir dollar. 'Thank you,' she said with equal
casualness, deliberately lowering her eyes so that he
wouldn't see that glow of pleasure in them. It was

hardly the most lavish gift in the world, but Kent had given it to her, and that made it more precious than a dozen diamond necklaces.

Kent returned from the kiosk and handed her a large paper cup. 'Coke.'

'What else?' she grinned and drank the cold, sweet liquid quickly, secretly deciding that she would have much preferred a cup of tea.

'Come on.' He threw his empty cup into a nearby bin and raised a wry eyebrow. 'Duty calls.'

As soon as she arrived back in her hotel room later that afternoon, Jana submerged herself in a warm, scented bath and viewed the evening ahead without enthusiasm. Kent had told her to be ready by eight when they had parted in the foyer.

Jana grimaced, wriggling her aching feet in the soothing water. A party was just about the last thing she felt like in her present mood. She rested her head against the end of the bath and closed her eyes. Oh, why couldn't she have had this one last night alone with Kent? Was that too much to ask? she wondered despairingly. For tomorrow he was flying back to London—and she would be staying in Canada.

She stepped out of the bath, her eyes deep pools of misery as she openly accepted the decision she had made all those days ago. She wasn't going to fall into the same trap as her father; wasn't going to spend the rest of her life wanting what could never be hers. All that remained for her back in London was empty, endless evenings and weekends by the telephone, waiting for the call that would never come. She gritted her teeth. No, she was determined not to live her life that way. After tonight, Kent had to be banished from her thoughts, from her heart, from her life. If only, she thought for the hundredth time, she could have just had one last evening alone with him . . .

The party was even more of an ordeal than she had anticipated. She sat on a chair by the wall, foot tapping unconsciously to the loud beat of the music, her eyes fixed steadfastly on the swirling throng of dancers that filled the large hotel room that Ben had hired for the night.

Somewhere in that mass of bodies was Kent and by his side would be Rowena, in a backless, flame-coloured gown that in theory should have clashed with her hair, but in practice made the extrovert girl look even more vibrantly beautiful. In comparison, Jana felt safe and boring in her dress with the demure neckline, fitted bodice, and calf-length, softly gathered skirt. She had been attracted to the dress originally by the colour, the same deep green as her eyes, but now she wished that she had selected something a little more daring. More sexy was what she really meant, she admitted ruefully, and her mouth curved. In reality she would probably feel far too self-conscious in a dress that revealed quite as much bare skin as did Rowena's.

She caught sight of Kent then, his dark head bent over the tawny one, saw him smile in response to something Rowena must have said, and she felt as if she had been stabbed, so acute was the pain.

Kent had danced with practically every woman at the party, Jana acknowledged miserably—she being the one notable exception. In fact, she thought despondently, he seemed to have forgotten her very existence.

'Hi, mind if I sit here?'

Quickly, Jana turned her head and looked up at the fair-headed young man who had addressed her, recognising him immediately, although she had never actually spoken to him, having seen him in the Sinclair entourage over the last few days.

'I'm Pete Sinclair,' he introduced himself with an engaging grin, and then pulled a face. 'Yea, Ben's my uncle!'

'Jana Morton,' she murmured reluctantly, wishing he would go away, but he sat down next to her.

'I know,' he grinned. 'I've been wanting to catch you alone for days, but every time I get anywhere near you, that bodyguard of yours whisked you off somewhere else.'

'My bodyguard?' Her eyes flew open.

'Yeah.' He indicated the tall, dark-haired man standing just a few feet away. 'You and him got something going?'

'What?' Jana exclaimed, and shook her head quickly.

'Well, he sure is protective, that's a fact. I'd only have to look at you and I'd get the "no trespassing" sign.'

'You're wrong.' She started to giggle at the sheer absurdity of it all. 'He's my stepbrother.' She was unsure of what had prompted her to admit that.

'Oh, I see. Family. Well, I guess that explains it.' His brown eyes surveyed Jana with satisfaction. 'Least I've made you laugh. You were looking as if your pet dog had just been run over.'

'Oh.' She was confused and embarrassed to think that he had been watching her all evening. 'It's just so hot and noisy in here,' she said lamely.

'Awful,' he agreed and his eyes lit up enthusiastically. 'Hey, how about you and me clearing off and finding somewhere a bit quieter?'

Jana was just about to refuse, when out of the

corner of her eye she glimpsed Kent again and saw the
way his arm was now resting casually across Rowena's
bare, golden shoulders. Anything would be better
than sitting here like a masochist.

'OK,' she said recklessly, jumping to her feet,
deciding too, in that minute, that there was an
openness and honesty about the fair boy's face that
she instinctively trusted.

'Great!' He grinned delightedly. 'Hadn't you better
tell big brother that you're leaving?'

'No.' She shrugged. 'He won't even notice I've
gone.'

Jana sat on the edge of the swimming-pool, dripping
with water, and watched Pete perform a lazy
somersault, admitting that his cheerful,
uncomplicated companionship had lifted her spirits.

They had visited a small, quiet bar, and then he had
driven her back to her hotel, announcing out of the
blue as they drew up outside, 'Hey, this hotel has a
pool. Let's go for a swim.' His eyes had danced with
fun. 'I've got my trunks in the car.'

And she had been crazy enough to agree, Jana
acknowledged with a grin, knowing deep down that it
had been because she wanted to postpone being alone
for as long as possible, put off that moment when all
her thoughts would go racing back to Kent.

Pete swam to the side and pulled himself out. With
calm detachment, Jana surveyed the muscular
proportions of his superb, athletic physique. How
strange. She could look at this undeniably attractive
young man, clad in the briefest of swimming-
shorts—and feel nothing. And yet she had only to be
in the same room as Kent and she felt weak and
vulnerable, exposed to nerve-racking sensations.

'Guess what?' she smiled at Pete. 'We forgot to bring any towels with us. You'd better come up to my room to change.'

Grinning conspiratorially, they crept through the foyer, ignoring the disapproving glance from the receptionist as she caught sight of their wet, scantily clad figures.

Jana led Pete into her room. 'You can change in the bathroom,' she told him quickly. 'Oh, let me grab a towel first.'

When the bathroom door was firmly closed behind him, she stripped off her swimsuit and wrapped herself in the large hotel towel, wringing out water from her hair with one hand.

'Pete.' She thumped on the bathroom door. 'I'm going to ring down for some coffee. Want some?'

It was amazing how at ease she was with him, she mused, feeling none of the acute self-consciousness she would have experienced with Kent in similar circumstances.

She was only half dressed when there was a sharp tap at the door and, expecting room service, she draped the towel back round her and opened the door, her eyes widening as she saw Kent standing there, face like thunder.

'Where the hell have you been?' Before Jana had time to protest at the way he pushed past her into the room, the bathroom door opened and Pete emerged, white shirt unbuttoned, dark jacket slung casually over his shoulder.

'It's all yours, honey,' he called out and then paused as he saw Kent. 'Hi,' he smiled easily.

As if she were in a trance, Jana saw Kent, white-faced and tense, stride across to the fair boy's side, standing over him ominously.

'Out!' he said thickly.

'Hey, take it easy!' Pete held up his hands and with a shrug, turned towards the door, stopping to murmur over his shoulder, 'I'll call you tomorrow.'

For a moment Jana was speechless, her body trembling with anger and humiliation.

'How d-dare you!' she finally spluttered, and then her words became incoherent as Kent roughly grabbed hold of her bare arm and swung her in front of him, so that she was only inches away.

'What the hell do you think you've been up to?' he thundered. 'Going off with a boy you've never met, inviting a total stranger up to your bedroom?'

'He wasn't a stranger,' Jana shouted, eyes smouldering with all her pent up fury as she glared up at him. 'He's Ben Sinclair's nephew, as you damn well know.' Her eyes narrowed to slits of green fire. 'Is that what you think? That we've just been to bed together? Don't judge everything by your own standards,' she spat. 'We went for a swim, that's all.' Immediately she regretted offering him any explanation at all; he could think what he liked.

His mouth twisted, his eyes travelling to the damp, discarded swimsuit lying on the floor. 'I know.'

'And even if I had been to bed with Pete, it's absolutely no concern of yours,' she flared.

His grip on her arm tightened so hard that she nearly yelped out with pain.

'You're wrong, Jana. It is my concern.'

For a moment, her anger ebbed, confused by the strangeness in his voice, the dark, mysterious shadows in his eyes.

'Let go of my arm,' she muttered, 'you're . . .'

Her protest was abruptly halted as his mouth, hard, warm and demanding claimed hers. Jana's head swam, her eyes flickered closed, she was powerless to resist the cascading pleasure as his lips moved languorously down her throat, his tongue teasing the sensitive hollow at the base of her neck, his firm yet gentle hands caressing her bare shoulders and back in slow, sensual circles of shivering delight.

'Jana, I want . . .' he muttered brokenly. 'I want to make love to you.'

Stupefied, she gazed up into his face, the lean hardness of his body against hers a physical reflection of the desire in the heavy, dark eyes. A warning bell clanged in her head, clamoured for self-preservation.

'What?' Something inside her snapped. 'You ignore me all evening, can hardly be bothered even to speak to me . . . and then you burst into my room, throw out a . . . friend of mine . . . and then calmly announce you want to make love to me?' Her legs felt as if they were going to give way. 'What do you expect me to do? Throw myself into your arms with cries of gratitude and delight?' Her voice was choking. 'Go to hell, Kent!'

'You damn little idiot!' His eyes blazed into hers. 'Don't you know why I've been keeping my distance?' he demanded hoarsely. 'Do you think it's been easy, when all I wanted was . . .' The words died in his throat as his mouth covered hers again, his hands moving over her body seducing her mind, lowering all her defences. She was incapable of thinking about anything but that desperate yearning inside her that was making her move instinctively against him, feeling herself drown in the torrent of pleasure that threatened to engulf her completely.

'No!' With all her strength, she pushed him away from her. He had not spoken one word of love, had given no indication that he even cared about her; he wanted her simply to satiate a physical need.

'Jana, what's wrong?' he asked huskily.

'I've just had enough of being mauled about by you,' she choked out. She saw the shooting dart of confused pain flicker in his eyes, but couldn't stop herself from adding viciously, 'What happened then, Kent? Rowena turn you down?'

For a second she thought he was going to strike her, but then he turned abruptly and walked out of the room.

Jana remained rooted to the spot, staring after him with stunned eyes. The knowledge that Kent was physically attracted to her, that he desired her, gave her no pleasure. It was no consolation when she wanted to be loved by him. She started to shake, hot, scalding tears stinging her eyes and then, as if she was in a dream and nothing was real any more, walked across the room and picked up the telephone.

Some fifty minutes later, Jana picked up her suitcase and closed the bedroom door behind her. Silently she moved down the carpeted corridor to the next room, and stooping down, pushed a white envelope under the door.

She stood up, ashen-faced, and took a step backwards, completely oblivious of the suitcase behind her.

'What the devil . . .' The door was flung open and Kent, still fully dressed, gazed down at the prone figure, his eyes immediately taking in the case.

'Going somewhere?' he enquired brusquely, helping Jana none too gently to her feet.

She swallowed. 'I called Andrew. He's coming over to collect me straight away.'

'At this time of night?' Kent's dark eyebrows shot up.

'He stays up working until four,' she explained rapidly. She, too, had been astounded that Andrew should offer to come over immediately when she had falteringly told him of her decision. Perhaps, she decided drearily, there had been something in her voice that had alarmed him.

'So you've made up your mind,' Kent said quietly, and she nodded unhappily.

'I've just come to say goodbye,' she mumbled, desperately hoping that he wouldn't see her letter until after she had gone and learn that she had intended taking the coward's way out. But her wish wasn't granted as he suddenly bent down and picked up the envelope, turning it over in his hand. His mouth twisted but he made no comment.

'What about your flat?' he asked.

'I'm going to write to the landlord and ask him to send the rest of my things on.' She had most of her possessions with her anyway.

'I'll come down and wait with you until Andrew comes,' he offered quietly.

'No!' She couldn't bear to say her final farewell to Kent in front of anyone else.

There was a long silence, green eyes fixed on the craggy face, trying to commit every detail of the harsh, beloved features to memory forever.

Slowly, Kent extended a hand and gently touched the side of her face.

'Be happy, Jana,' he muttered gruffly.

She nodded, not trusting herself to speak, and then, eyes dark with anguish, gave him one last look and turned away. There would be no tears; she had none left to shed. There was no pain even, just numbness, as if part of her had died.

CHAPTER SIX

'I DON'T expect you to give me an answer straight away,' Pete Sinclair said quietly, looking across at the slim girl sitting on the bank of the creek beside him, dangling her bare feet into the clear, rushing water, soft brown hair falling over a bare, sun-tanned shoulder like a silky curtain. Remnants of their picnic lunch were strewn on the grass around them. 'You can't be surprised . . . you must know how I feel about you.'

As Jana turned her head and gazed directly into his face with cloudy green eyes, he asked incredulously, 'You really didn't know? We've been seeing each other for a year now, and you didn't have a clue?'

She hesitated. 'I knew you were fond of me,' she said awkwardly, 'but . . .' Marriage! Perhaps she had been deliberately ducking the issue, but it had never occurred to her that Pete should want to marry her.

He jumped to his feet agitatedly. 'The trouble with you is that you can't take anything seriously. You treat life as if it's one big joke. Nothing matters—not even me!'

'Pete, that's not true!' Jana denied hotly, aghast at the uncharacteristic outburst from the blond boy, but deep inside her she wondered with shock if he was right. She pushed the thought away immediately. She had long ago stopped the painful and unproductive habit of analysing her emotions and thoughts. 'Lots of things matter to me—Andrew, you, my job.' She frowned, staring straight ahead over the creek to the dense pine forest on the other shore. Flying J. land as far as the eye could see, and beyond lay the mountains, their peaks shrouded today by low, scudding white clouds.

Pete slumped down beside her again, the anger ebbing from his good-natured face.

'I'm sorry, Jana, I don't know what got into me then.' He sighed. 'I shouldn't have said anything today—but I guess I just wanted to stake my claim before you go to London tomorrow.' He grimaced. 'I don't like the idea of some English smoothie muscling in while I'm not around.'

'Hey,' Jana murmured gently, trying not to grin at his ridiculous and unwarranted fears. 'I'm only going to be away a few days.' She lifted her feet from the water and wriggled her toes in the sun to dry.

'I know.' He paused, and then added in a rush of words, 'I just wish you weren't going at all.'

'I can't let Andrew down,' she told him quietly, absent-mindedly pulling on her socks and riding-boots. 'He's not exactly overkeen on going himself. You know how he hates publicity. But the film première is in aid of charity so he can't possibly not go. After all, the film is based on one of his books.'

'Yeah,' Pete nodded. 'I know I'm being unreasonable. Course you've got to go with him.' Swiftly he reached out and caught hold of Jana's small hands in his larger ones and looked at her earnestly. 'You will think about what I've said while you're away? About us.'

'Y-yes, of course,' she said uneasily, wishing desperately that it had never come to this, that their easy-going, casual relationship could have continued unaltered. She shook herself mentally. She had been burying her head in the sand to think that Pete would be happy with the status quo forever. She was very fond of him, enjoyed his company, but she knew with dismal certainty that her feelings ran no deeper. But then, Jana thought with a dip of her stomach, she wasn't sure she was capable of deeper feelings for anyone any more.

'I know you're not in love with me,' Pete said quietly as if reading her thoughts, 'but we do get on really great together, we have loads of fun—and we're good friends. It's not a bad start.' He was silent for a moment and then added softly, 'I'd take care of you, Jana. For always.'

It was on the tip of her tongue to protest loudly that she didn't need anyone to take care of her, that she was perfectly capable of doing that herself, but she couldn't be that cruel. 'Yes, I know you would,' she said quietly instead. Pete Sinclair was offering her everything she had once dreamed of—a home, security, love—and she knew with cold certainty that she was going to refuse it.

'Pete——' she said slowly, but he cut in abruptly.

'No, I don't want your answer yet. Wait until you come back from England.' He tried to grin. 'Maybe you'll find you missed me like crazy.'

She nodded, knowing that she was only putting off the inevitable, but weakly she was grateful to do so. Slowly she began to collect up the debris from their picnic and stow it neatly in her saddle-bag.

'You'll be seeing that Kent guy again in England, won't you?' Pete suddenly blurted out and Jana, caught off guard, deliberately concentrated on fastening the saddle-bag before casually answering.

'It's possible. His agency have been handling all the PR for the film studio.' So that was what had been bothering Pete.

'I never did manage to figure out what was going on between the two of you,' he said slowly.

Jana shrugged. 'Nothing.' She gave a nonchalant grin and added honestly, 'Certainly not on his part, anyway. I was very immature in those days, Pete. I'd never even had a proper boyfriend. Kent was about the first man I'd had anything to do with and so, for a while, I thought I was in love with him.'

'And now?' His eyes were intense.

'And now?' she repeated brightly. 'There is no now. Kent belongs to the past. Whatever I felt, or thought I felt, is gone.' She lapsed into silence, reluctant to pursue a conversation about Kent. She had faced the fact that she might see him again with calm equanimity—at least she thought she had, but that unexpected thud of her heart when Pete mentioned his name troubled her.

Anxious to lighten the situation, she stood up and threw the saddle-bag over her shoulder.

'Race you to the ford,' she challenged, and was relieved to see the grin that sprang to Pete's face.

'You're on!'

She darted over to the dun-coloured mare grazing near by, tightened the girth with deft hands, gathered up the reins and swung easily up into the saddle. After a year's patient tuition from both Andrew and Pete, she was now a competent horsewoman.

It was early evening when they arrived back at the ranch, the sun sinking behind the tall, coniferous trees casting dappled shadows over the large, solid house that had been built by Andrew's father. And her grandfather, Jana reminded herself with a smile.

'Staying for supper?' she asked Pete as they turned the horses out into the corral by the side of the house.

'No, thanks,' he refused with a smile. 'I guess you've still a million and one things to do yet.'

'I've not finished packing,' Jana admitted, following the fair boy over to his pick-up truck. She was grateful when he made no reference to their earlier conversation, but merely kissed her lightly before clambering up into the truck.

'See you soon,' he yelled out as he started off down the dusty track.

She waved back, watching until he had disappeared from view. Why couldn't she fall in love with Pete? It would make life so easy, so safe and uncomplicated.

Sighing ruefully, she walked round to the back of the house and discovered Andrew stretched out in a wicker chair under the veranda, his eyes closed. She smiled, deciding not to disturb him, and walked into the house and up the wide staircase to her bedroom.

An open suitcase lay on the cream carpet in the middle of the room; clothes waiting to be packed were arrayed on the cream and peach bedspread where she had placed them that morning.

Jana had a quick shower in the modern en suite bathroom, changed into a clean pair of jeans and T-shirt, and started her laborious chore. She ought to take at least one thick jumper, she decided, and, moving across to a wooden chest, she began to sort through her winter clothes. She fished out a red jumper and stiffened as her action disturbed a small silver coin nestling beneath it. Slowly, she picked up the coin, her fingers curving around its smooth edge. A hot summer afternoon . . . Calgary Stampede . . . and Kent . . . Abruptly, she opened her hand, letting the dollar fall from her fingers, the defence mechanism she had built up over the past year sharply forcing the memories from her mind. Memories that belonged to the past, to another girl, in another life.

Jana walked with confident grace by her father's side
as they emerged from the Customs Hall at Heathrow
and faced the barrage of flashlights and a
bombardment of questions from waiting reporters. It
was ironic, Jana mused wryly, that the more Andrew
shunned publicity, the more he seemed to attract it,
his very reticence seeming to stimulate public
curiosity.

'I didn't expect all this,' he muttered, and she
smiled reassuringly up at him, knowing how much he
was loathing it all, and did her best to fend off the
fatuous questions being thrown at him herself.

More than one male head turned for a second glance
at the slim figure with large, arresting green eyes who
moved with calm composure by the side of the tall,
gawky man.

The deceptive severity of Jana's light blue summer
suit emphasised rather than disguised the feminine
lines beneath, her body no longer that of a girl but of a
young woman, the soft curves disciplined into firm
tautness by tennis and riding in the summer and
skiing and skating in the winter. The hours of outdoor
activity were reflected, too, in her clear, honey-tinted
skin, the glow of her face owing nothing to artificial
aids.

Jana valiantly tried to conceal her growing
impatience as the Press continued to badger them,
irritated by the fact that they seemed more concerned
with her father's personal life than with his
professional one. She was sorely tempted to reveal
with a confiding smile that Andrew kept a harem of
nubile maidens locked up in his basement, only
releasing them from their chains on Saturday nights

for his weekly orgy. That ought to satisfy them!

Somehow, Andrew became separated from her and she was disconcerted to find that all the attention was now being directed at her. Then out of the blue, she heard a clear, male voice.

'Is it true that you are in fact Mr Jameson's illegitimate daughter? That you never even knew of your father's existence until a year ago?'

'What was it like to discover that your natural father was a famous, wealthy man?'

Jana turned white as the Press seemed to close in on her, their questions becoming more and more insistent. Desperately, she unsuccessfully tried to push her way through the human barrier in front of her. Then she suddenly felt a firm hand on her elbow, guiding her miraculously through her tormentors towards the exit.

Gulping a deep breath of fresh air to steady her voice, Jana looked up at her rescuer for the first time.

'Thank you, Kent.'

Her first instinctive thought was how little he had changed over the past year; the dark, craggy face and the brilliant blue eyes had lost none of their impact. Jana's face was schooled into an expression of impassiveness, a calmness totally belied by her inner turmoil, the sharp constriction of her throat, the dip of her stomach. With a feeling of sick inevitability, she acknowledged that she had been deluding herself to imagine that time would have made her immune to this compelling man. She had a sudden, insane desire to run away from him, to rush back into the terminal and board the first available flight back to Canada. But instead she held out a hand and said, as calmly as if she were greeting a guest for dinner, 'How are you, Kent?' She permitted herself a distant little smile. 'I wasn't expecting you to come and meet us. It was very kind of you.'

'Oh, it was no trouble, I can assure you,' he mimicked her precise, stilted voice, and Jana, braced for the mockery in the glinting blue eyes, was momentarily dumbfounded to realise that he was studying her with open appreciation.

'You've changed, Jana,' he murmured, his eyes lingering caressingly over her slim body with an intimacy that fired the blood coursing through her veins. But the past year had stood her in good stead; she had become an expert at concealing her emotions. Her face remained a polite mask, her eyes expressionless as she said lightly, 'Have I?'

'Come on, Jana, you don't need me to flatter you. I'm sure your charms haven't passed unnoticed by the male populace of Calgary.'

'No,' she murmured sweetly. Damn him. Did he think she had been trying to flirt with him? 'I have to call out the Mounties at least twice a week to clear the path to my door.' However she had expected Kent to react at seeing her again, it certainly hadn't been like this. She felt as if he was playing a game with her, a game to which she didn't know the rules. But she would learn, Jana thought, that was for sure.

'Where's the car?' she asked briskly, stooping to pick up her small travel case, but Kent was there before her, his fingers brushing her hand as she snatched it away. She frowned, trying to ignore the tingle that had shot up her arm at that briefest of contact, wondering if it had been deliberately engineered by Kent.

'I'm parked just over there,' Kent murmured, placing an arm casually across her shoulders as he guided her along. 'Cold?' he asked solicitously, and she knew that the sudden tensing of her muscles beneath his hand had not gone unnoticed.

'Yes,' she answered evenly. 'I should have remembered what English summers are like.'

She slipped into the passenger seat of the dark blue saloon as he held the door open for her, only too conscious of the interested gaze on the length of her sun-tanned, bare leg revealed as her skirt rumpled up. Meeting his eyes evenly, she pointedly straightened the skirt, pulling it down over her knees.

'Pity,' he commented tauntingly. 'I was enjoying the view.'

'I should hate you to be distracted while you're driving,' she returned equably.

He gave a low chuckle and walked round behind the car to the driver's side, Jana unable to resist watching him undetected in the wing mirror. Then her hand flew to her mouth in horror.

'Where's Andrew?' she demanded as Kent slipped in beside her. It was impossible—but she had forgotten her father's very existence. It took every ounce of control to stop the colour flooding her face as she looked into Kent's mocking eyes.

'He's gone straight to the television studio in a taxi.'

'What?' she exclaimed. 'He's hardly set foot in England and you whisk him off for an interview!'

'Stop behaving like a mother hen, Jana.' Kent turned on the ignition and manoeuvred the car out of the parking-space. 'Andrew agreed to this interview months ago. No one's pressed him into doing anything.'

'I didn't know anything about it,' she muttered, aggrieved.

'Maybe he just forgot to tell you.' He shot her a quick sideways glance, dark eyebrows raised infuriatingly. 'Does he have to get a late pass if he goes out at night?'

She didn't answer. What on earth were they arguing about Andrew for? She looked steadily out of the window as they left Heathrow and headed for London, outwardly relaxed, sitting back casually in her seat, but inside her nerves were taut and brittle. Heaven help her—ten minutes with Kent had reduced her to this quaking mass of jelly, making her oblivious to everything, even her own father!

He must have come straight from the office, she mused, since he had been clad in a suit when he met her. He had now discarded the jacket and tossed it carelessly across the back seat, and rolled back the sleeves of his crisp white shirt. Involuntarily, her eyes strayed to the tanned, muscular forearms, the afternoon sun glinting on the sheen of fine, dark hairs.

'Well, how's your love-life?'

She stared, totally disconcerted by the question he had flung at her with the same casualness as if he were enquiring if she still took sugar in her tea.

'That is none . . .' Swiftly she changed tack. He had been deliberately trying to rile her; well, she wouldn't give him the satisfaction of an indignant outburst. Instead she said huskily, as if recalling many cherished moments, 'Wonderful, Kent, just wonderful.'

She saw the black eyebrows shoot up but without being able to gauge the expression in his eyes couldn't be sure if it reflected his amusement or surprise.

'Still seeing Pete Sinclair, then?' he drawled.

She gave him a baffled glance. 'How on earth . . .?'

He cut in easily. 'Cindy told me last time I was there that you'd been over with Pete a few times.' He paused and added thoughtfully, 'That was in

May—you were in Vancouver at the time, I believe. And when I was over there last December you'd banished yourself to Montreal.' He drew up at a set of traffic lights and turned his head, blue, inscrutable eyes scanning her face. 'Where had you planned to disappear to next time I visited Canada? Australia?'

Green eyes gazed back into the blue ones unflinchingly. 'Are you trying to imply that I've been deliberately trying to avoid you?' Jana asked evenly.

'Haven't you?' His voice was flippant but his eyes had darkened.

'Why on earth should I?' she retorted steadily, and added sweetly, 'The lights have changed, Kent, dear.'

Of course she had been avoiding him! Each time Cindy had told her of an impending visit from Kent, she had deliberately planned her vacation to coincide with it, sick with fear that if she saw him again the whole tortuous process of trying to obliterate him from her mind would have to start all over again. But that had been at the beginning, Jana reminded herself briskly; now she was completely cured from that sickness. She admitted honestly that his physical attraction had not lessened—but on an emotional level, she decided confidently, she was now indifferent to him. He would never be able to hurt her again; there was nothing to be afraid of any more.

She concentrated on watching the road, smiling as they passed familiar landmarks. It was good to be back in England, though she wondered now if she would ever want to return permanently. She had grown to love the country of her birth.

Kent drew up outside the Chelsea mews cottage that had been rented for the duration of Jana and Andrew's visit, the latter having an intense dislike of hotels.

'It's delightful,' Jana murmured appreciatively as she stepped into the small, sunlit hall.

'Do you want me to take those upstairs?' Kent asked, indicating the two suitcases he was grasping, Andrew having evidently deposited the luggage in the car boot before he'd sped off in a taxi. It was most odd that he hadn't even waited to tell her where he was going, Jana thought, not for the first time.

'No, just leave them in the hall, Kent, thanks.'

'I'll show you round,' said Kent, starting down the hall. 'The kitchen's through here. I think you'll find the fridge is pretty well stocked up.'

'It's all right,' said Jana hastily, following him quietly. 'I'm sure you must be in a hurry to get home.' Then, feeling churlish, she added, 'Would you like a drink?' She held up the duty-free carrier bag. 'Whisky? Or coffee?' Even to her own ears, her voice sounded reluctant and ungracious.

'Coffee, please,' he answered, as she edged past him into the kitchen. 'If it's not too much trouble,' he added ironically.

'Nothing's too much trouble for you, Kent,' she retorted sweetly, plugging in the electric kettle.

'Cut it out,' he drawled, leaning casually against the door jamb. 'Cups and saucers in the cupboard to your left.'

She poured boiling water on to the instant coffee and turned her head. 'Milk?' she asked innocently.

'Black, please.'

'Sugar?'

'Damn it all, Jana,' he muttered tersely, taking a step towards her. 'You know how I drink my coffee. You've made enough for me.'

'That was a long time ago,' she said deliberately, handing him a cup, uneasily aware of how close he was to her.

His eyes never wavered from her face, as wordlessly he took the proffered cup and placed it on the small kitchen table.

Jana couldn't move, felt herself mesmerised by the blue eyes and, as the dark head bent towards her, knew with heart-stopping certainty what was going to happen. She willed herself to relax, and received the warm, hard mouth with cool, impassive lips, neither responding nor flinching away.

'Suddenly find me totally irresistible?' she enquired flippantly as he lifted his head, her tranquil expression betraying nothing of her emotions. She prayed that he wouldn't hear the erratic thundering of her heartbeat, which sounded to her own ears as loud as the massed band of the Royal Marines.

His eyes were dark and inscrutable as he searched her face, and then he grinned carelessly. 'Just thought it was about time we said hello properly.' He picked up his coffee and drank it in one long gulp.

'I'll see you to the door,' Jana said immediately, not caring if she did sound rude, the desire for him to be out of the house overriding everything else.

'How kind.' He raised a mocking, dark eyebrow and walked down the hall, saying over his shoulder, 'I'll pick you up at eight-thirty. That should give you enough time to unpack and have a bath.'

Jana stood stock still, staring at the broad back. 'Sorry?' she said stiffly.

He swung round, suddenly seeming to dominate the small hall. 'I've booked a table at Marcel's for nine. You'll like it there.'

'Oh, really?' How could he be so impossibly arrogant as just to assume she would fall in with his arrangements like a meek little lamb. 'Aren't you taking rather a lot for granted? I may have already made plans for this evening.'

'What?' She nearly laughed at the expression on his face, and then he smiled, 'Jana, would you have dinner with me tonight, please?'

She smiled back sweetly. 'Will Rowena be coming, too?'

'Rowena?' His eyebrows shot up.

'Your inseparable companion,' Jana quoted drily. 'I hear that congratulations are in order.' She could have bitten off her tongue with chagrin; she hadn't meant to sound so stiff—and concerned!

'You shouldn't believe everything you read in the scandal sheets,' he retorted crisply. 'Oh, I was forgetting, you're in that line yourself now. I hear Andrew managed to wangle you a job on the local rag.'

'Andrew did not "wangle" a job for me!' she said hotly. 'I got it on merit. And the *Post* is hardly a "rag".'

She cursed inwardly. She had allowed Kent to needle her, break through her composure.

'So you take your job pretty seriously, then?' he asked, a strange note in his voice.

'I love it.' She was the most junior member of staff, a trainee reporter, the general dogsbody, but she thrived on it, determined to succeed at her new career. She watched Kent's face curiously, wondering at the sudden brooding darkness in his eyes, but couldn't help herself from reverting to their original topic.

'So it's not true that Rowena is finally going to make an honest man of you?' she asked lightly, but her stomach muscles clenched, waiting for his answer.

'No.' He gave a wolfish grin. 'We're just loving friends,' he said with great deliberation.

'Still just the one hobby, then?' she responded sweetly.

He ignored the caustic comment and opened the front door.

'See you at eight-thirty.'

She shook her head, her hair sweeping across her shoulders. 'Thanks for the invitation, but no.' She smiled. 'I'm sorry. You'll just have to cancel the table or find someone else.' That shouldn't present many problems, she thought wryly. 'Goodbye, Kent.'

She shut the door after him and leant against it, conscious that her legs were trembling, conscious, too, that she was relieved and yet illogically disappointed that Kent hadn't found it necessary to say goodbye 'properly'.

After unpacking, Jana submerged herself in a hot, scented bath, but felt too restless to linger long in the water and, drying herself quickly, donned a pair of jeans, still her favourite casual wear. Not bothering with a bra, she pulled a soft white angora sweater over her head, brushed her hair vigorously, and tied it back in a ponytail.

Barefoot, she returned downstairs and entered the small living-room, immediately switching on the television, flicking from programme to programme, uncertain as to what channel and what time her father would be appearing. That was something, she reminded herself wryly, she should have remembered to ask Kent.

She sat down on the sofa, curling her legs under her, and grimaced. It was humiliating to have to admit it but from the moment she had first seen Kent at the airport everything else had been dispelled from her mind. It had been the unexpectedness of seeing him that had thrown her, she convinced herself. She

hadn't been mentally prepared, having expected that
she wouldn't be seeing him until the following
evening at the film première, where, no doubt, he'd
appear with Rowena Fenner clinging to his arm.

It was ironic that Rowena, her career both in
modelling and acting having taken off since her
Freedom girl days, should have been cast as the
female lead in the film of Andrew's best-selling
thriller.

Jana jerked herself upright, eyes glued to the
television set as an unknown male presenter
announced Andrew Jameson. Then came a shock as
the cameras swung across to her father, sitting beside
a tall, slim girl with long, tawny hair.

So that was why Kent had invited her to dinner,
Jana decided ruefully—Rowena had been otherwise
engaged.

Unconsciously, her hands gripped the arm of the
sofa, nervous for Andrew, but her apprehension
proved to be unfounded. Her father looked relaxed,
answering the questions put to him with ease, even
recounting the odd amusing anecdote. Jana sighed
with relief and turned off the television as the
programme came to an end. Would Andrew have
eaten or would he want to go out for a meal when he
arrived back from the studio? Why had she refused to
have dinner with Kent? The question that had
taunted her all evening sprang to the fore again, and
once more she deliberately left it unanswered.

Jumping to her feet, she wandered into the kitchen
and inspected the store cupboards. She could always
make herself an omelette, she supposed without much
enthusiasm. And she could have been sitting in a
candlelit restaurant with Kent.

Why had she gone through that childish charade of

pretending that she had forgotten how he drank his coffee? There was nothing she couldn't remember about Kent, right back from the first time she had met him at boarding school.

She sat down on a stool and buried her head in her hands. Who had she been trying to fool? A year hadn't solved anything—the moment she had laid eyes again on that harsh, craggy face, heard the deep, familiar drawl, she had known with terrifying clarity that she still loved Kent.

She had spent the last year trying to convince herself that she wasn't going to fall into the same trap as her father, but it had all been for nothing. She knew why she would never marry Pete—or anyone else. She would never accept what would inevitably always be second best. If she couldn't be with Kent, she would rather spend the rest of her life alone.

She raised her head and stared drearily into space. Avoiding Kent didn't help; seeing him was even more painful. Her knuckles clenched into white fists. She had tried so hard, so desperately hard to rid herself of him, had almost convinced herself that she had been successful, acting out her role as the carefree, happy-go-lucky daughter of Andrew Jameson. But Pete had seen through the charade. He had been right; she couldn't take life seriously any more, not once the most important part of it had gone. Kent was, and always would be, the most important thing in the world.

It took several seconds for her to realise that the telephone was ringing and several more to discover its whereabouts. She recognised Andrew's voice immediately.

'I watched the interview. You were terrific,' she told him enthusiastically.

He laughed. 'It wasn't too bad, was it?' He paused. 'I've asked Rowena to have dinner with me. Why don't you jump in a taxi and come over and join us?'

'I think I'll have an early night, Andrew, thanks.' Her appetite had vanished over the past five minutes. 'Enjoy yourself,' she added quickly. As soon as she replaced the receiver, she regretted her decision, a wave of depression settling over her as she realised that she would now be alone for the rest of the evening, with too much time to think. By rights she ought to be feeling jet-lagged and tired by now, but the adrenalin seemed to be surging round her body, setting her nerves on edge, making it impossible to go to bed or even settle down in the living-room with a book. She prowled round the cottage, finally pausing on the upstairs landing to stare out into the gathering gloom.

She didn't know how long she stood there, but when she eventually broke from her reverie it was dark outside. She was just about to draw the curtains, when in the glow from the street light she made out the familiar blue saloon pulling up outside. A few seconds later the doorbell rang, barely giving her time to compose herself, to try to calm that erratic beating of her heart.

Slowly, Jana made her way downstairs, and taking a deep, steadying breath, flung open the front door.

'Hello, Kent. Can't you keep away?' she greeted him flippantly, her whole body tingling at the sight of him in dark, slim-fitting trousers and a black, open-necked shirt. If it were possible, he looked even more devastatingly masculine.

'As Andrew seems to have deserted you, I thought you might be feeling lonely,' he said, brandishing a bottle of red wine. 'Unless of course . . .?'

His eyes taunted her and she knew it would be useless to pretend that she was expecting anyone else, especially when she had only arrived back in London a few hours ago.

'Come on in,' she said lightly. 'I'll fetch some glasses.'

She darted into the kitchen and counted to ten slowly, and then, armed with glasses and a corkscrew, returned to the living-room.

Kent was standing by the empty fireplace, leaning casually against the mantelpiece, and as Jana moved across the floor to hand him the corkscrew she was acutely conscious of his lazy scrutiny, knowing instantly from the gleam in the lingering blue eyes that her bra-less state had not passed unnoticed. To her shamed horror, she found that her traitorous body was responding to the narrowed, interested gaze, and she prayed desperately that the hardening nipples couldn't be detected under the camouflaging sweater. But that teasing smile curling at the corners of the firm mouth told her that she might just as well have wished for the moon. She wanted to rush from the room, mortified that one look from Kent could so visibly excite her. With iron control she forced herself to walk nonchalantly over to the sofa, aware that his eyes had never once left her.

'You know that Andrew has taken Rowena to dinner, then?' It took tremendous effort to keep her voice on an even keel; it was even harder not to keep looking at him.

He shrugged. 'Mmm. I've been over to the studio.'

To see Rowena?

'Thanks.' She accepted the glass of wine he handed her, and tried not to stiffen as he sat down next to her on the sofa, one arm resting casually across the back of the sofa, his hand uncomfortably near her head.

'Don't you mind?' she asked, turning her head slightly so that she could see his face.

'Why should I?' he said easily. 'I don't have any claim on Rowena, nor she on me. She's perfectly free to see whoever she chooses—as I am.'

'The ideal relationship,' Jana commented drily, knowing that for her that type of relationship would be far from ideal.

'It has its advantages,' he said smoothly. 'No emotional ties, no dramas, no one gets hurt.'

She studied her hands as if she had never seen them before. She couldn't imagine anyone ever getting close enough to Kent to be able to hurt him. She jerked her head up and smiled sweetly into his face.

'Isn't your male pride wounded? I mean, being passed over in favour of an older man?' Was his relationship with Rowena really as casual as he professed?

'I thought Rowena was having dinner with Andrew—not setting up home,' he said sardonically, and then lifted a dark eyebrow. 'What's the matter? Disappointed that I'm not going to challenge your father to a duel at dawn?'

'Don't be ridiculous!' She swallowed a mouthful of wine without even tasting it. She might have known how useless her attempt to provoke him into revealing his feelings would be.

'There's only ever been one person I'd consider worth fighting for.'

Her eyes flew to his face, puzzled by the strain in his voice, the ambiguity of his words, the deep intensity in his voice. And then she understood.

'Kent,' she said quietly, her eyes transfixed to the craggy face, 'tell me about Chrissie.'

CHAPTER SEVEN

'CHRISSIE,' Kent repeated slowly, his eyebrows furrowed across his forehead in a dark line, the muscles clenching in the strong jaw.

Abruptly, he turned his head away from Jana, but not before she had glimpsed those shadows in his eyes. She studied the craggy profile in silence, awash with shame that she was forcing him to relive a past that was so obviously still painful, merely to satisfy her own curiosity.

'Kent, I'm sorry . . .' she started hesitantly.

'Maybe I should tell you about Chrissie.' He cut through her words, his voice so low that she had to strain her ears to hear him. 'How much do you know?' He turned his head again, blue eyes drawing and holding the green ones.

'I just know what Cindy once told me,' Jana said tentatively. 'That she committed suicide.'

'Suicide? Is that what Cindy told you?' His voice rasped.

'Well, not exactly,' she stammered, trying to remember exactly what the Canadian girl had said all that time ago. 'But she said Chrissie took an overdose, so I just assumed . . .'

'She never meant to kill herself—I'm sure of it!' he said brusquely. 'It was a classic cry for help. Except I wasn't there to help her.'

'Don't tell me any more,' Jana blurted out, not being able to bear the anguish in his eyes, the tearing pain and bitterness in his voice.

For a moment he remained silent and then said quietly, 'I want to tell you, Jana.' Unexpectedly he moved his arm and gently took hold of her right hand, grasping it firmly with his own. 'It was the summer I graduated from college. Jake was on his honeymoon, and his parents had gone to Vancouver for the weekend, so I was staying in their home so Chrissie wouldn't be left alone.' He paused, his eyes darkening until they were almost black. 'One evening, Chrissie and I were just sitting in the kitchen, talking, when out of the blue she told me she'd been having an affair with a married guy, and she was going to have his baby. She had told him and he had more or less told her to get lost.' Kent's face was ashen. 'I just saw red. I didn't want to hear any more. I just charged out of the house.' He released Jana's hand abruptly. 'I didn't come back till dawn . . . and I found Chrissie. I called the ambulance straight away, but it was too late.'

'And you've been blaming yourself all these years,' Jana said softly, her heart aching for him. 'Kent,' she said sharply, 'it wasn't your fault. You were hurt.'

'What?' His eyes narrowed. 'I wasn't hurt, Jana. You've got it all wrong. I wanted to kill the bastard who had hurt Chrissie. She was so naïve, so young . . . Jake would have felt exactly the same way.' His eyes bore into Jana's. 'I didn't love Chrissie, not in the way you think. I'd known her all my life. Hell, you don't think her parents would have left me in the house alone with her if I hadn't thought of her as a kid sister!' His eyes were tormented. 'Chrissie trusted me, and I let her down.' His knuckles were white. 'She needed someone to talk to, and I walked out on her. But I was so angry.'

'You couldn't have known what she'd do,' Jana said softly, wanting desperately to ease his sense of guilt.

'I should have stayed with her,' he said stonily. 'Made her realise it wasn't the end of the world, that everything was going to be all right. Her parents were nice folk—they'd have stood by her.' He raked a hand through his head. 'She was only seventeen.'

'But if she'd felt that desperate she'd have only tried some other time, when no one was around. You can't blame yourself.'

'You still don't understand, do you?' he said hoarsely. 'It wasn't a suicide attempt, there was no note, nothing. She expected to be found in time. By me . . . only I came back too late.'

Jana felt sick with pity for the young, confused girl whose life had ended so tragically, but even stronger was her compassion for Kent, and the overwhelming longing to comfort him.

'I'm so, so sorry.' Her eyes were awash with tears, not just for Chrissie but for the man she loved.

For a second he remained as still and as expressionless as a granite statue, and then swiftly he pulled Jana on to his lap, pressing her so tightly against his chest that she thought she would suffocate. As his hold lessened, her arms went instinctively around his neck, her hands curling through the unruly, dark hair.

Wide, vulnerable eyes gazed into the craggy face, drowning in the deep blue of his eyes, and in that imperceptible moment the atmosphere between them changed, became charged with electricity.

Gently Kent's fingers touched her face, traced the contours of her cheekbones, her skin burning under his touch, and slowly outlined the curve of her mouth.

His head bent towards her and then she was lost in a swell of pleasure as his mouth came down firmly on hers.

When Kent had kissed her earlier, it had taken every ounce of self-control to remain calm and impassive; now the tender warmth of his heated kiss broke through all her defences; she was powerless to resist, every pore in her body alive to Kent.

As he raised his head she felt momentarily bereft, and then realised he was deftly releasing her hair from the confining ponytail, letting it fall around her shoulders, twisting a silken length through his fingers.

'It's so beautiful,' he murmured huskily, his mouth tracing a scalding path down her neck, his hands moving from her hair to her breast, caressing each firm contour through the soft sweater.

Jana arched against him, aching to feel his hands on her bare, heated skin, her breathing erratic as she sought his mouth again, her hands unbuttoning his shirt and eagerly touching the hard male flesh beneath.

'Hello, Jana. I'm back.' There was a sharp crash as the front door slammed shut.

'I don't believe it!' Kent forced himself upright, his breathing unsteady as he fastened his shirt.

'Andrew.' Jana turned a flushed face to her father, conscious of how she must look with her disarrayed hair tumbling down her back and her crimsoned cheeks. Her embarrassment increased as she saw the comprehension in the soft brown eyes. 'D-did you have a good meal?'

'Andrew.' Kent nodded casually, and Jana was surprised that he made no attempt to rise to his feet to greet the older man, and then, as she turned her head and surveyed the long, lean form, she understood the reason for his apparent discourtesy. Almost choking with trying to suppress her laughter, Jana scrambled to her feet and rushed from the room, mumbling something about making coffee under her breath.

She had wasted the entire day, Jana thought with self-disgust as she emerged from the shower with a towel wrapped around her.

'Bathroom's free,' she called out to Andrew, and vanished into her bedroom. She sat down on the edge of the single divan and began to towel her damp hair vigorously.

'See you tomorrow,' had been Kent's parting words when he left last night, soon after drinking his coffee. Jana scowled. And she had hung around the cottage all day like a lovesick teenager, waiting for him to telephone, not daring to go out in case she should miss his call. She had even deluded herself that he might just turn up on the doorstep the way he had the previous night. The only consolation was that at least Kent would never know what a fool she had been.

Sighing, she stood up and went across to the white wardrobe and fetched her dress, pulling it over her head. Turning round, she inspected herself anxiously in the wall mirror and sighed with relief. In the V-necked, figure-hugging black robe, with her newly washed hair cascading down her back in soft, gleaming waves, she looked young and alluring. She carefully applied a faint touch of make-up to her tanned skin and fastened the simple silver chain with the black opal, a present from Andrew on her twenty-first birthday, around her neck.

Her father would have nothing to be ashamed of in

her appearance, she decided. Large green eyes gazed back mockingly at her. In her preparations for the evening ahead, it hadn't been Andrew who had been uppermost in her mind.

'You look lovely.' Andrew smiled up as he watched his daughter walk down the stairs towards him. 'You'll be the most beautiful woman there tonight.'

'I think you might be just a little bit biased.' She grinned at him, thinking how distinguished he looked in his dark evening suit. He had spent most of the day with his English publishers, not returning to the cottage until late afternoon. 'I'll go and fetch my handbag. The taxi should be here any minute.'

She found it difficult to concentrate on the film, her eyes peering into the dark auditorium, scanning the seats in front of her for a glimpse of a familiar head, but without success. She had half expected Kent to arrive with Rowena, but the latter, looking stunning in a silver-grey sheath dress, had been escorted by a tall fair-headed man.

She forced her attention back to the screen but seemed to have completely lost the thread of the story.

Why hadn't Kent telephoned her today? Perhaps he had been too busy . . . Who was she trying to kid? How long did it take to pick up a phone? No, Kent hadn't called because he hadn't wanted to. She had been insane even to expect that he might. The only reason he had come to see her last night was that he'd been at a loose end without Rowena. She had merely been a pleasant diversion, that was all. She closed her eyes. Surely he would be at the party to be held later at the well-known London hotel? And then what?

She flicked open her eyes and to her horror realised

that the credits were appearing on the screen.

'What did you think of it?' She turned to Andrew brightly.

'Er—very good,' he murmured vaguely, and Jana guessed what a strange experience it must have been for him, to see the characters of his imagination being brought to life.

She linked her arm through his in a sudden burst of affection. 'Come on, Dad, let's go and grab a taxi before they all go.'

He smiled down at her and murmured gently as they hurried towards the exit door, 'Do you know, that's the first time you've ever called me Dad?'

'I think I shall have to sit this one out,' Jana said desperately as she was whirled frantically around the huge hotel ballroom by a perspiring young man. She wasn't even sure of his name; the moment she and Andrew had walked into the party, he had rushed to her side and swung her into the throng of gyrating dancers. And that had been half an hour ago.

'Right you are,' he agreed amiably, releasing her from his grasp. 'Catch up with you later.' He turned away and waved a hand in the direction of a small, vivacious blonde girl. 'Sara, darling.'

Sighing with relief, Jana edged her way towards the open french windows leading out on to a patio, longing to be out in the fresh air, away from the thundering music, and drunken, shrill voices around her. She had lost sight of Andrew long ago.

'Been abandoned already?' a deep, familiar voice drawled in her ear.

'Of course I haven't been abandoned,' she said irritably, her eyes widening at the sight of Kent in a dark suit, the cut across his broad shoulders superb. 'I just didn't feel like dancing any more.' The catch in her voice could be attributed to breathlessness, she decided quickly. 'Did you enjoy the film?' she added lightly.

'I didn't attend the première,' he answered brusquely, confirming her suspicions. 'Who is he?'

'What?' She frowned, puzzled for a second, having completely forgotten about her energetic dancing partner. 'I haven't a clue,' she said carelessly.

'Just someone you picked up?' His eyes glinted like ice.

'That's a revolting thing to say!' She stared up into his thunderous face. 'This is a party, for heaven's sake, not a street corner in Soho!' She changed tack quickly and smiled sweetly. 'What's the matter? Bad day at the office, dear?'

'Shall we dance?' he said brusquely, ignoring her sarcasm, and before Jana had time to gather her wits she found herself in his arms, being guided skilfully across the floor in time to the slow, languid beat.

She forgot everything as the hand on her back increased its pressure, forcing her towards him across the slight distance that separated them. Her senses reeled as her body was moulded into the lean, hard form, her eyes unable to move from the craggy face above hers.

'Do you realise this is the first time we've danced together?' he suddenly murmured in her ear, and for the first time that night Jana saw a smile touch the straight mouth.

She simply nodded, not trusting herself to speak, and just gave herself up to the pleasure of being in his arms, hardly aware that he was manoeuvring her across the room towards the open french windows.

Nothing mattered any more except this moment in time. Then vaguely she was conscious of the line of fairy lights flickering above her and the hard stone flags under her feet.

'Kent,' she murmured absently, 'we're . . .'

The remainder of her words were never uttered as his mouth abruptly took possession of hers. Her head spun under the suddenness of the onslaught, her legs no longer supportive but useless lumps of jelly.

There was none of the tenderness or gentleness of the previous night in that kiss, but a fierce, demanding hunger, his hard mouth crushing hers savagely as his hands snaked around her slim hips, drawing her into him.

He lifted his head, and the blood drained from Jana's face as she registered the dark, burning intensity in his eyes.

'Come on,' he muttered hoarsely, 'let's get out of here.'

'N-no,' she protested feebly as he grasped her hand roughly and propelled her back through the french windows and the packed room beyond.

'I can't leave Andrew,' she mumbled desperately as she was marched through the hotel foyer and out into the car park. 'He'll worry.'

'He'll guess you're with me,' Kent grunted, almost bundling her into his car.

It was only as he started the engine that Jana seemed to come to her senses, and with mounting horror she realised that her weak passive resistance to Kent's whisking her off unceremoniously like this would almost certainly be taken by him as acquiescence to whatever he had in mind for the next few hours. And that, she thought with a skip of her heart, would hardly be a bedtime mug of cocoa at his flat.

'Kent,' she finally found her voice, 'take me back to Chelsea, please.'

'No.'

She stared at his face but it was impossible to determine his expression in the darkness. He had to be joking.

'Where are we going, then?' she asked trying to sound unconcerned. 'Your flat?' Her hands gripped the edge of the car seat as if her very life depended on it.

'My cottage in the New Forest. You and I have some unfinished business.' He paused as if to make sure his words sank in. 'And this time,' he added with great deliberation, 'I don't intend to be interrupted.'

She flinched at the cold calculation in his voice, his meaning only too apparent. Was that how he saw her—'unfinished business'? She wasn't even aware he had a cottage in the New Forest.

'I can't resist it when you woo me with soft, tender words,' she muttered caustically, eyes staring out into the darkness, trying to quell the mounting panic within her. He was teasing her, she reassured herself quickly, and then her heartbeat quickened as she saw they were heading out of London.

'Look, if this is some sort of game,' she said, her nerves twanging, and then she gave a cry of alarm as he slammed on the brakes and ground to a halt.

'You think this is a damn game?' he demanded harshly, one hand on the back of her head, jerking her towards him. His mouth settled possessively on hers, and his free hand began to move down the length of her body, caressing each soft curve with intimate, expert fingers. To Jana's humiliation, she found her body responding to his touch, arching up against him, her mouth feverishly seeking his.

'Right!' He pushed her away abruptly. 'Have I made my point?'

'Oh, you've made your point all right!' The words were torn from her as she sat trembling by his side, her mind a whirlpool of confusion. She clenched her teeth together in an effort to stop the tears from gathering in her eyes, and didn't even know why exactly she was crying—or trying not to cry. A strange feeling of apathy crept over her. What did anything really matter? She flicked a glance at the silent man beside her and her mouth twisted wryly. Why be a hypocrite? She wanted Kent as much as he evidently desired her; it was useless to deny that. It was time she stopped living in cloud-cuckoo-land and faced up to reality, treated this whole situation with the same cold, unemotional objectivity as Kent. But he had had more practice, she reminded herself bitterly.

She chewed the tender skin inside her mouth until it was sore and gazed blankly out into the shrouded countryside. At least Kent was honest, she thought dully, making no false promises, not uttering any insincere, meaningless words of love. She closed her eyes. There were two quite simple alternatives: she could create a scene, demand Kent return her to London, or she could passively go through with it. So why was she hesitating?

'You've gone very quiet, Jana. What's the matter? Belated feelings of guilt about Pete?' He cut through her confused thoughts brusquely.

It took her a second even to realise who he was talking about, and then she saw it as her way out.

'Yes,' she agreed quickly. 'He trusts me, he'd be so hurt.' Pete was going to be hurt eventually anyway, she thought unhappily, hating herself for using him as an excuse.

'I'm sure he'll understand one minor indiscretion.'

Minor indiscretion!

'Some people believe in being faithful to each other,' she snapped. 'Something I doubt you'd understand.'

'I'm always faithful to one woman at a time,' he refuted her comment calmly, overtaking a car with ease.

'Until she bores you, I suppose,' Jana muttered caustically. Did that mean that his relationship with Rowena was over? 'And how long do you think it'll be before you become bored with me?' she asked with saccharine sweetness, too late realising she had used the present tense. 'As I'm only going to be in England a few days, I should say the odds are pretty much in my favour.'

He shrugged, seeming immune to her sarcasm. 'There's nothing to stop you coming back to live in England, is there? I dare say I can help you find a job. Not working for me, obviously.'

'Obviously,' she repeated drily. 'Can't possibly mix business with pleasure—and I presumably would be categorised as pleasure.' This was fast bordering on the farcical. Surely Kent couldn't be seriously proposing that she return to England to become his mistress? 'Of course I'd have to think about it. Weigh up the pros and cons.'

'Cut it out, Jana,' he interrupted curtly. His voice deepened. 'This isn't a joke.'

'What?' The blood drained from her face and her heart hammered wildly beneath her rib-cage. 'My word, you're arrogant!' Her voice shook. 'You expect me to leave my home, my friends, my job, just . . .' She broke off in a choking gasp. Just to be with a man she loved more than life itself—until he grew tired of her.

'Yes?' he prompted quietly.

'Go to hell!' she muttered savagely, turning her head away, hardly registering that they had now turned off the main road and were driving along a dark, narrow, winding lane. Her anger, born out of hurt, subsided as quickly as it had erupted, leaving her feeling cold and empty. A year ago, she realised drearily, she might have been tempted by Kent's proposition, convincing herself that it was merely a prelude to a permanent commitment. But she wasn't that naïve any more. A few weeks, maybe months with Kent might be worth a lifetime with any other man—but it would leave her emotionally scarred for life.

The car slowed to a crawl and in the glow of the headlights Jana saw a pony standing with its head lowered lethargically in the middle of the road. Saw it hazily through that sudden burst of fear swallowing her up. Which was irrational and ridiculous, common sense admonished her. There was no need to be afraid of Kent! She wouldn't be a prisoner in his cottage, and the New Forest was hardly the wilds of Scotland. She could leave whenever she chose, which, she decided adamantly, would be first thing in the morning. Even if Kent refused to drive her back to London, there were train and coaches. She frowned. Damn it, she only had some small change in her bag, certainly not enough for her train-fare. Oh well, Kent would just have to lend her the money.

'Planning your escape route?' His mirthless low chuckle set her teeth on edge. It was disconcerting, too, to realise how easily he had read her erratic thoughts. 'Here we are, home sweet home.'

Despite her tension, Jana's interest quickened, and she stared out of the window, wishing that she could see more in the darkness. The car bumped over a cattle-grid and went up a tree-lined drive. Then, peering through the gloom, Jana could just make out a large, red-brick house, which became more discernible as Kent played the car lights on to it.

'It's hardly a cottage,' she commented.

'It was two keepers' cottages originally,' he explained, bringing the car to a halt. 'But it's been knocked into one.'

She climbed out of the car and followed him up to the front door, picking her way carefully in the pitch darkness.

'No neighbours?' she asked, unable to see any comforting lights around them.

'There's a farm just down the lane, but it's in a hollow and so you can't see it from here.' He flicked on the hall lights. 'Come on, I'll show you around.'

Jana couldn't stop her growing delight as he silently led her from room to room. Whoever had converted the two cottages into its present, single, immaculate state had done so with imagination and skill. It retained all its original charm and character, the necessary modernisations having been executed with sympathy and as unobtrusively as possible.

'Think I've made a good job of it?' Kent asked idly as he led Jana through into the living-room.

'You did all this?' she demanded wonderingly, her eyes roaming around the room, taking in the well-stocked bookcases, the comfortable leather armchairs, the landscape paintings on the cream walls, visualising it in the winter months with a roaring fire in the huge brick fireplace.

'I did have some help,' he said casually, 'but basically yes.'

'It must have taken you ages!'

He nodded ruefully. 'I spent every weekend I could down here.'

Jana gazed at him, thinking once again how little she really knew about the man she loved. He could well have afforded to have the cottage restructured and modernised professionally, and yet he had elected to undertake the mammoth project himself. And, she admitted, done it superbly.

'How can you bear to leave it and go back to London?' she asked quietly.

'It's becoming increasingly difficult,' he admitted, and then grinned. 'Maybe I'll buy a helicopter and commute each day.'

She laughed. 'Build a helipad on top of the agency roof?'

'Why not?' he said lightly, his face perfectly serious. 'I'll show you upstairs.'

'R-right,' she agreed uneasily and he flicked her a quizzical glance, sensing her reluctance, and then gave a low, mocking laugh.

'Oh, I see. Upstairs equals bedrooms!' He took a stride across the room until he was standing only inches away from her. 'You think I'm like one of Pavlov's dogs, hm? One sight of a double bed and I'll turn into a raving sex maniac!' He shook his head disbelievingly.

'Of course I don't!' Jana retorted stiffly. 'But you hardly brought me down here to admire your DIY skills at this time of night, did you?' she added scathingly.

'You think I have a set time of day for making love?' he demanded caustically. 'My goodness, Jana, you must have an exciting sex-life!'

'You're disgusting!' she snapped. 'And it's none of . . .'

'Yes, I know. It's none of my damn business anyway.' He suddenly looked weary, raking a lean hand through his dark hair. He took a stride towards the door, pausing to say over his shoulder, 'You can sleep on the sofa if you feel safer downstairs.' Jana flushed at the mockery in his voice. 'Though personally I think you'll find it a great deal more comfortable in the spare room.'

'The s-spare r-room?' she stammered, gazing at him with wary green eyes.

'Stop looking at me like that,' he muttered tersely. 'What do you think I'm going to do? Force myself on you?' His mouth twisted. 'That would hardly be a pleasurable experience for either of us, would it?' He walked out of the room, and, subdued and totally bewildered, Jana followed him into the hall and up the wooden staircase.

He pushed open the second door on the landing and stood aside to let her enter first. Jana didn't even glance around the room; her eyes were riveted on the pile of clothes lying neatly in the centre of the bed.

'But those are my things!' Her eyes widened with shock. 'How did . . .'

'I collected them this evening while you were at the film première,' he cut in coolly. 'Andrew gave me a key this afternoon when I met him.'

She was too stunned to speak for a second. Andrew had known what Kent intended—it was impossible to believe. 'You went into my bedroom and rummaged through all my personal things?' she finally demanded, outraged.

'I have seen female underwear before,' he returned drily. 'And I didn't rummage through anything, just brought the whole lot, as you can see.'

How could he stand there, leaning casually against the door, looking so relaxed and unperturbed?

'You planned the whole thing . . . kidnapping me,' her voice rose.

'Don't over-dramatise,' he cut in sardonically. 'I hardly gagged and bound you! As I recall, you came along willingly.'

'I did not!' she denied hotly, the betraying colour scalding her face as she met the cynical smile. She should have refused point-blank to leave the party with Kent right from the start, never been so weak as to allow things to go this far.

Slowly she walked across the thick beige carpet to the bed and touched the familiar clothes. Why had Kent gone to all this trouble anyway? It was all so incomprehensible.

'I don't understand . . .' She found herself voicing her confusion out loud.

'Why I'm not demanding that you share my bed for the night?' he cut in drily. 'I've told you. I'm prepared to wait until you come to me willingly.'

A tremor shivered down her spine. 'And you think I might become more—willing?' She groaned inwardly at the tremor in her voice, wanting desperately to appear as cool and composed as Kent.

'That's a risk I shall have to take, isn't it?' he said calmly. 'Pleasant dreams,' he added mockingly, and, turning abruptly on his heel, left the room.

Jana sat down on the bed before her trembling legs gave way, staring at the closed door with dark, agitated eyes. Her head was like a merry-go-round, spinning faster and faster, out of control. She was going to explode; she wanted to scream, to shout out her pain and confusion. She wasn't even aware she was crying until she tasted the salty tears on her face. Burying her head in the pillow to muffle the noise, she began to sob in earnest.

CHAPTER EIGHT

'THOUGHT so,' Kent said calmly, putting the dictionary down. 'There's no such word. Try again.'

In a swift movement, Jana jumped to her feet and quite deliberately scattered the letters all over the Scrabble board.

'Oh, dear, how clumsy of me,' she said innocently.

'Temper, temper,' he chided her mockingly.

'Which side of the bed did you get out of this morning?' His eyes gleamed. 'Now if you'd climbed out of *my* bed . . .'

'Shut up,' she ordered him crossly and moved across the living-room to the window, watching the sheeting rain lash against the panes.

'Want some coffee?' Kent asked lazily, pushing his chair back. 'Or would you prefer something a little stronger to settle your nerves?'

She ignored his taunt. 'I'd like to phone Andrew,' she muttered.

'To reassure him you're in safe hands?' he enquired drily.

She threw him a withering glance over her shoulder, fighting down that overpowering urge to slap his sardonic face.

'Right, I'll put the kettle on.' He rose to his feet and strode from the room.

Jana didn't pick up the telephone immediately but remained staring moodily out across the immaculate lawns to the open forest beyond, hardly registering the spectacular view.

It wouldn't be so bad if she could get outside for that ride that Kent had promised once the weather cleared up, but being cooped up with him like this was fast driving her mad.

She had tossed and turned all night and woken feeling irritable and depressed, and discovering Kent in the kitchen whistling noisily as he tended a pan of sizzling bacon had not exactly improved her mood.

'How many eggs?' he enquired cheerfully, hardly glancing at her as she stood frowning in the doorway, clad casually in her jeans and green T-shirt.

'I'm not hungry,' she said, sweeping her hair back over her shoulder, as she perched herself on a stool by the round wooden table. 'Just coffee, please.'

'Help yourself,' he said easily, cracking two eggs into the pan for himself. 'Sleep well?'

'Like a log,' she returned evenly, but her eyes narrowed as they studied the broad, denim-clad back suspiciously. Had he heard her prowling restlessly around her room in the early hours? No, she dismissed the idea with a scowl as he began whistling again. Nobody could be that cheerful first thing in the morning if they hadn't slept solidly all night. Her mouth twisted wryly. So much for her disturbing proximity in the adjacent room! Mechanically she poured coffee into a cup and stared down into its cloudy depths.

How could he look so relaxed and impossibly good-humoured when she felt a mental and physical wreck, her nerves as taut as a steel wire, her eyes sore and gritty from lack of sleep? She shot his back a baleful glance and then lowered her eyes quickly as he sat down opposite her and began eating his breakfast with relish.

'I had planned that we go for a ride this morning,' he told her casually, swallowing a piece of bacon. 'But it's a bit pointless getting drenched.'

'I didn't know you had a horse.' But then, she reminded herself with a bitterness that appalled her, there seemed to be a million and one things she didn't know about this man.

'Mmm. I bought a chestnut mare a couple of months ago. I keep her stabled at the farm down the lane when I'm not here. I've arranged to borrow one of their ponies for you this weekend.'

'How kind!' Jana muttered tetchily and then frowned. Her clothes in the spare room . . . this pony on loan . . . It was all so organised, she thought resentfully, hating the feeling that she seemed to be losing control over her own life.

'Pour me a coffee, would you, please?' Kent said casually, his eyes glinting as they rested on her flushed face. 'According to the weather forecast, the rain should ease off later, so I think we'd better postpone our ride until this afternoon.' He paused, blue eyes taunting her. 'Which means we have all morning to kill. Any ideas?'

'How about playing Scrabble?' she returned caustically.

'You must have read my mind.' He grinned at her
sceptical face. 'Now, where did I put my Scrabble
set?'

Jana picked up the telephone, dialled the number and
then replaced the receiver before the line was
connected. She drummed on the table with her
fingers. She had no need to tell Andrew where she was
as it would appear that he had been perfectly aware of,
and in fact had condoned, Kent's plan to bring her
down to the New Forest. So what was she actually
going to say to Andrew anyway? Go into raptures
about the wonderful time she was having in the
country? Her mouth twisted bitterly. What was the
matter with her? She could walk out of the door and
go back to London right now, as had been her original
intention last night. But that had been when she was
under the impression that Kent was going to spend
the entire weekend pressurising her into going to bed
with him. So why wasn't she relieved that he had
evidently changed his mind? She scowled savagely.
Instead she just felt irritable . . . and so damn
frustrated! And worst of all, she had a strong
suspicion that Kent knew exactly how she was feeling
and was loving it, toying with her like a cat with a
mouse. A shiver tingled down her spine as she
recalled his words about waiting until she came to him
willingly.

'Damn, damn, damn!' she cursed out loud.

'Problems, Jana? Can't you get through?' Kent
appeared, stooping slightly as he came through the
door, bearing two mugs of coffee, and Jana squirmed
inside as she met his innocent expression.

'No,' she muttered. 'I'll try again later.'

He raised a quizzical dark eyebrow but didn't pursue the subject. 'Stopped raining,' he announced cheerfully, handing her a mug.

Jana's spirits rose as she cantered along a track in the open forest behind Kent, the wind invigorating in her face. The sky overhead was a soft, watery blue, the wet grass beneath shimmering under the increasingly powerful rays of the midday sun. They came into a clearing and reined the horses to a halt, pausing to watch a newborn foal make its first valiant attempts to master its long, ungainly legs.

'Who do they all belong to?' Jana asked curiously, her eyes roaming around the other mares and foals scattered about.

'Anyone who has forest rights can graze their animals,' Kent explained. 'Not just ponies, but cattle, donkeys, pigs.' He sat erect in the saddle, eyes narrowed against the sun, and Jana felt her throat constrict at the sheer vital beauty of the man and horse.

'Time we were going back,' he said, turning the chestnut mare homewards. Her eyes still fixed upon him, Jana hardly concentrated on her own, smaller grey pony, as it automatically turned to follow the other horse, and then felt it stumble beneath her. As if everything was in slow motion, she began slipping from the saddle. Vainly she attempted to regain her balance, clutching at the saddle, but to her abject humiliation she heard the gentle thud as she landed on the ground. She was winded for a second and then sat up to find Kent standing over her, the reins of both horses in his left hand, a broad grin on his face.

'I might have been killed and you just stand there laughing!' she snapped, glaring up at him with flashing, green eyes.

'Hardly,' he said, watching her scramble to her feet. 'You were only going at a snail's pace and the ground is as soft as a mattress after all this rain. The only thing you've injured is your pride!'

She scowled and with great deliberation limped over to the grey pony, biting her lip for greater effect.

'Oh, don't trouble to give me a leg up,' she murmured with a brave little smile. 'I can manage.'

'Fine.' Kent smiled, and, flicking a pair of reins towards her, swung himself easily back into his own saddle.

Jana scowled at the lean, retreating figure, and then moved off at a brisk trot to catch him up.

'Ankle still painful?' Kent enquired, the sympathy in his voice belied by the gleam in his eyes.

'Very.' Jana winced, hobbling in front of him through the cottage back door, having just returned from turning out the horses in the field down the lane.

'I'd better take a look at it, then.' Before she could protest, he placed a hand on each side of her shoulders and pushed her down on to a stool.

'Now, which ankle was it?' he asked innocently, squatting on his haunches by her side.

'The right one.' She stiffened as he deftly pulled off her boot and removed her sock, praying against

all hope that somehow her ankle would miraculously be revealed as a lurid mass of blue-yellow
bruises.

'Looks all right to me,' he murmured, his eyes
moving up to her face, the slim, creamy ankle
still held lightly in his left hand. Then slowly
and deliberately his hands moved under her jeans,
his fingers languorously smoothing the silken
calves.

'Kent,' she choked, mesmerised by the blue eyes
gazing deep into her own, a nerve beginning to beat
erratically at the base of her neck.

'Yes?' His voice was low, almost muffled, his
fingers never pausing in their slow, sensuous
strokes.

'I . . .' She broke off in a stifled gasp as he abruptly
rose to his feet and pulled her up against him, his
hands resting possessively on her hips, drawing her
into his hard thighs.

'Do you want me to make love with you?' he asked
harshly, his mouth only inches above hers. His eyes
intent, dark with desire, held hers, making it
impossible to look away, impossible to deny the
clamouring of her restless body. At the same time, a
fierce hatred spurted over her that he was forcing
her to acknowledge openly that burning ache within
her.

'Yes.' She forced the word out and then was only
conscious of the overwhelming relief as his mouth
finally came down on hers.

All her dammed-up hunger and frustration came
flooding out as she feverishly returned his kiss, her
hands stretching up to his shoulder as she arched

against him.

Swiftly he picked her up in his arms, carried her into the living-room and deposited her gently, full-length on the rug by the empty fireplace.

He dropped to one knee beside her, his eyes lingering slowly over every curve and plane of her body.

'I want to see, touch, kiss every inch of your beautiful body,' he muttered hoarsely, his hands moving intimately over her jean-clad thighs, sliding upwards under the blue T-shirt, easing it over her head. Deftly he released the front clip of her lacy bra, and, the blood moving like treacle through her veins, Jana felt the warmth of his mouth on her breast, his tongue flicking sensuously over the tautening nipple, then moving over to capture the other, throbbing rosy peak.

Jana held herself against him, her head thrown back with aching pleasure as his lips moved down across the soft silkiness of her stomach to the waistband of her jeans. As she heard the rasp of her zip, she wound her arms around his neck, helping him to ease the cumbersome clothing over her slim hips, sighing her intense delight as his fingers slid beneath the lacy briefs, teasing, stroking, caressing until they reached the pulsating, heated moistness of her innermost being.

She gave a small groan, her hands reaching up to unbutton his shirt, desperate to feel the hard flesh beneath, her fingers trailing the line of fine, dark hair over the taut, flat stomach until it disappeared beneath his jeans, her eyes imploring him to remove the remaining hindrance between them.

She heard the rustle of clothes and then felt his knee move between her legs, pushing them gently apart as he came to lie between her thighs, his mouth claiming hers, his tongue probing between her lips, a mirror of the urgency in the hard loins moving rhythmically above her.

'I've waited so long for this.' Kent's voice was ragged as he curved his hands under her hips, lifting her up to meet him. Her initial gasp of pain as the fragile barrier between them was finally separated swiftly turned to one of dazed delight, as wave upon wave of nerve-tingling sensations swamped her fevered body. She was drowning, melting as she felt Kent move inside her. There was nothing else in the world, only this man driving her with him to unscaled heights of tearing pleasure.

She bit her lip to stop the gasp as her whole body shuddered its release, Kent's voice muffled against her breast as he groaned his heated satisfaction.

She clutched him tightly against her, wanting the world to stop so that she could stay like this forever. Then, as she slowly opened her eyes, she came back to harsh reality, the shock of what had just happened, what she had wanted to happen, shuddering through her. For Kent it had been just one more enjoyable physical experience, whereas for her it had been the inevitable culmination of her love for him. Her hands fell to her side and, eyes dark with agony, she stared up at the ceiling.

'Jana?' he enquired softly, propping himself up on one elbow, stroking a damp tendril of hair from her forehead.

She lowered her eyes to blank out his face. 'You're hurting me,' she mumbled, pressing her hands against the hard chest.

'I'm sorry.' The moment he moved off her, she sat up, stretching out a hand to retrieve her scattered clothes.

'What are you doing?' He had rolled over on to his stomach and was looking up at her, frowning his bewilderment at her frantic efforts to cover her nudity, his eyes dark as they scanned her tense face. 'What the hell's the matter?' he demanded forcefully.

'I'm getting dressed.' She stated the obvious in a sharp voice. 'And then could you call me a taxi? I want to go back to London.'

'I see.' She saw his face whiten and with a swift, fluid movement he rose to his feet and walked with sure-footed grace to collect his clothes, totally unselfconscious in his nakedness. But then, why should he be embarrassed? Jana thought with a lump in her throat as she watched him from under her lashes. His lean, powerful body was superb.

'I'll go and pack my things,' she muttered, feeling utterly wretched. They should still be in each other's arms, murmuring tender, loving words, not staring at each other with frigid faces, speaking in harsh voices.

She walked towards the door and stiffened as she heard Kent demand caustically, 'If you've been seeing Pete Sinclair for the past year, why . . .?'

'Was I still a virgin?' she cut in coldly, knowing that sooner or later he had been certain to ask. 'Because

Pete happens to think there is rather a lot more to a relationship than just sex!' she spat out.

'Poor bastard!'

'What?' Her chin jerked up and she held her ground as she met the cold, narrowed eyes.

'Were you waiting until he proposed, Jana? Was that it?' he demanded harshly, his mouth twisting unkindly. 'What a shame you can't go on using your virginity as a bartering weapon!'

'That is a disgusting thing to say!' she stormed. 'But exactly what I might have expected from you!' She strode to the door and hurled back over her shoulder, 'As it happens, Pete has already asked me to marry him!' She slammed the door behind her with all her strength.

She ignored the longing just to throw herself down on the bed and sob, and rapidly threw all her possessions into the small suitcase in which Kent had evidently transported her belongings down there. She went into the bathroom, bathed her face in cold water and dragged a comb through her hair. She didn't even attempt to apply any morale-boosting make-up, knowing it would be useless. Her hands were trembling too much.

Chin raised, she marched back down the stairs and then halted as she saw Kent in the hall, a jacket slung over one shoulder.

'Taxi should be here in ten minutes,' he said shortly. 'Slam the door behind you when you leave.' He moved towards the front door.

'Kent!' she cried out, taking the remaining stairs two at a time. 'Where are you going?' Wasn't he even going to see her off?

'Out.' He turned to face her, eyes blank and unreadable. 'Enjoy the rest of your stay in England.'

She stared at him, unable to believe that expression of total indifference on his face. Didn't he care about her at all? If he had been furious it would have been painful enough, but this casual unconcern was unbearable. She stiffened, her face rigid, her eyes as blank as his.

'Thank you,' she murmured coolly, and swallowed. What did she say now? Thank you for a lovely weekend? Her mouth tightened, and then there was no need to say anything, because without even glancing back over his shoulder he had gone.

Afterwards, Jana could never remember the taxi-drive back to London. It was just a meaningless blur of jumbled countryside and towns. She sat in the back, staring straight ahead, not thinking, not even feeling. She was totally numb.

She came back to reality as the taxi pulled up outside the Chelsea mews.

'I won't be a moment,' she told the driver quickly. 'I'll just get the fare.'

'All taken care of, miss,' he told her. 'On Mr Tyson's account.'

'Oh, I see. Thank you,' she said, not having the energy to argue. Did Kent have a standing order with the taxi firm to take his female guests back to London when he had tired of them? she wondered drearily as she fished out her door-key from her handbag.

She heard a sound from the kitchen and found

Andrew pouring steaming water into a teapot.

'Jana,' he turned round and smiled. 'I've just been trying to ring you at the cottage. I had no idea you were on your way back. Where's Kent?'

'I've come back on my own,' she said casually, averting her eyes. It was on the tip of her tongue to ask how on earth he could have approved Kent's plan to take her down to his cottage, but suddenly that didn't seem important any more. She took a deep breath. 'I'm going back home, Andrew, tonight. I checked before I left the cottage. There's room on the last flight.'

'I see,' he said quietly, and Jana understood what she loved most about this unassuming man. It was the way he accepted everything she did without question; he never criticised her, never demanded an explanation or tried to force a confidence. It took every ounce of control not to burst into tears and throw herself into his arms, seeking reassurance like a small child. But she wasn't a child, and nothing would ease that ache inside her.

'Want me to come and see you off?' he asked gently.

'No.' She shook her head adamantly. 'I'll go and ring for a cab.'

'Are you feeling all right, love?' The plump, middle-aged woman paused in her collection of the dirty crockery and glanced down at the ashen-faced girl sitting alone at one of the cafeteria tables.

'Sorry?' Jana focused glazed eyes at the concerned, kindly face. 'Er, yes, I'm fine.'

'Well, you look proper poorly to me.' The woman shook her head disapprovingly. 'You shouldn't be travelling on your own.'

'I'm all right, really,' Jana said more firmly. Please go away, she thought desperately. Please leave me alone. 'I'm going to get another coffee.' She jumped to her feet as the other woman didn't move.

'Sit down. I'll get it.'

Her mouth opened and closed, her eyes widening with shock as they gazed up at the tall, dark-haired man. Vaguely, she was aware of the waitress moving away. 'You'll be all right now, dear.'

'What are you doing here, Kent?' Jana blurted out finally, gazing hungrily into the craggy face. Would she ever stop loving him? 'How did you know where I was?'

'Andrew told me,' he said briefly, sitting down opposite her. 'I telephoned to talk to you and he explained you were flying back to Canada tonight.'

'And you came straight down to the airport?' she asked in a small, bewildered voice.

'I was so furious with you earlier on, but when I'd cooled down . . .' He shrugged. 'I didn't want us to part as enemies, Jana.'

'No,' she agreed dully. How could Kent ever be her enemy? she wondered drearily.

'I've a present for you,' he said abruptly, bringing out a small bottle from his pocket. 'I had intended giving it to you this weekend, but,' his mouth twisted wryly, 'things didn't turn out quite as I planned.'

'Perfume?' Jana asked, frowning down at the bottle, immediately recognising the exclusive French label.

'Thank you,' she said quietly, puzzled why he thought it necessary to give her a gift. Did he honestly think she wanted or needed anything to remember him by?

'Aren't you going to try it?' he demanded.

She had the urge to throw the bottle at his head, but instead, weakly, she unfastened the small gold top and held the bottle under her nose.

'It's not being marketed until next month,' Kent told her. 'The agency is handling the promotion. What do you think?'

'It's very nice,' she muttered. She couldn't go through this agony much longer. 'I must go. I'll miss my flight.' Then she stiffened as he reached across the table and put a hand under her chin, forcing her to look up into his eyes.

'How would you describe the fragrance?' he demanded.

'I . . . er . . .' She couldn't think straight, drowning in the blue gaze.

'How about unique, haunting, unforgettable, enchanting . . .'

'Hardly original,' she managed to croak. Was he mad, making all this fuss about a bottle of perfume—when her heart was breaking?

'It's going to be called Jana,' he said softly, his fingers caressing the side of her cheek.

'I don't understand.' She looked at him with huge, bewildered eyes, her face burning under his touch. 'After . . . me?'

'Unique, haunting, unforgettable, enchanting,' he repeated very deliberately. 'For pity's sake, surely you realise why . . . I couldn't think of any other way to make you understand that . . .'

'Are you trying to say you love me?' she choked.

'You know I do!' he growled.

'No,' she protested weakly.

'Of course I do!' he muttered. 'Why else would you be the only woman I've ever taken to the cottage . . . my home. I wanted you to see it, wanted it to be your home too.'

'But all those things you said to me on the way down?' She stared at him, still not daring to believe he was serious.

'I was a bastard to you,' he admitted with a sigh, and took hold of her hand gently in his. 'But you were so damn cool and unapproachable. I thought at least I might get some reaction.' He shrugged. 'I thought if only I could just have you to myself for a couple of days . . . and instead you've ended up hating me.'

'Hating you?' she cried. 'But I love you, Kent. I've always loved you. You must know that.'

He searched her face. 'You mean it?' he asked tentatively.

'How can you even doubt it for a second?' she asked softly, her eyes awash with love.

For a moment green and blue eyes were locked together, oblivious to everything around them. Then Kent leapt to his feet. 'Come on, Jana.' He grinned, looking down into her glowing face. 'I refuse to propose in the middle of Heathrow Airport!'

The sofa in Kent's flat was a far more comfortable place to accept a proposal, Jana decided contentedly some time later, her arms wrapped around Kent as he lay stretched out beside her.

'How long have you loved me?' she murmured, nuzzling his throat, wanting to say those magical words over and over again.

'Always, I think,' he smiled, his arm tightening around her. 'I liked that skinny schoolgirl who came waltzing into my life and announced that she was glad I was her new father.'

'Oh, don't remind me.' She blushed at the memory.

'Then,' he paused to kiss her tenderly, 'when you came to work for me, I was appalled to discover that my feelings towards you weren't exactly brotherly any more.'

'You mean all that time we were in Canada?' she asked breathlessly.

'It was so difficult not to touch you!' His mouth curved wryly. 'Too difficult at times.'

'That first night . . . in the suite . . .'

'I stayed at a friend's,' he explained, guessing at her unspoken question. 'A male friend,' he added teasingly, and then his expression sobered. 'I didn't trust myself to sleep on the sofa, knowing you were only a few feet away.' He groaned. 'Hell, it was bad enough that night you stayed in my flat.'

The revelation that this strong, invincible man should have so doubted his self-control where she was concerned made Jana's eyes darken with wonder.

'But why didn't you tell me all this before?' she asked unsteadily, thinking of all the misery it would have saved over the past tortuous year.

'I was so damned confused,' he said gruffly. 'I knew I wanted you but I couldn't or wouldn't accept that I loved you.' His eyes implored her to understand, to forgive him. 'You reminded me of Chrissie in so many ways, you were so naïve. I couldn't risk just having an affair with you, couldn't risk hurting you.'

'The way Chrissie was hurt,' she broke in softly.

He nodded. 'I was such a fool. The fact that I was so concerned about you should have told me how much I loved you!' He smiled ruefully. 'Then, when I came back to England, I couldn't get you out of my mind. I kept going back to Canada, trying to convince myself that it was to see Jake and Cindy, but knowing deep down that it was you I had to see again. Only you were always conveniently away.'

'Yes,' Jane admitted. 'But not for the reasons you thought.' She searched his face. 'But why didn't you even write to me?'

He grimaced. 'I wrote you hundreds of letters—and tore them all up. I didn't know what the hell to say.' He paused and added quietly, 'Maybe I was frightened of being rejected. Every time I saw Jake and Cindy, they told me how happy you seemed, how you were still seeing Pete Sinclair.'

'Oh, Kent.' She curled her hands through the thick dark hair, covering his face with small, heated kisses, loving him so much it hurt.

'Would you have gone back and married him?' he asked gently.

'No. There was never anyone but you—or ever could be.' She frowned, her eyes clouding. 'I shall have to go back and tell Pete. It's only fair.'

He nodded, pulling her even closer, moulding her against him. 'If I can bear to let you out of my sight again,' he muttered hoarsely in her ear.

'I won't be away long,' she reassured him huskily, her breathing unsteady as his mouth trailed down her bare throat. And after that, she thought with a swirl of scorching happiness, there would be no more goodbyes. It was the last coherent thought she had for a very long time.

2 NEW TITLES
FOR MARCH 1990

Jo *by Tracy Hughes.*
Book two in the sensational
quartet of sisters in search of
love…

In her latest cause, Jo's fiery
nature helps her as an
idealistic campaigner
against the corrupting
influence of the rock
music industry. Until she
meets the industry's
heartbreaker, E. Z. Ellis,
whose lyrics force her to think
twice. £2.99

Sally Bradford's debut
novel **The Arrangement** is
a poignant romance that
will appeal to readers
everywhere.

Lawyer, Juliet Cavanagh,
wanted a child, but not
the complications of a
marriage. Brady Talcott
answered her
advertisement for a
prospective father, but
he had conditions of
his own… £2.99

W⬥RLDWIDE

AND THEN HE KISSED HER...

This is the title of our new venture — an audio tape designed to help you become a successful Mills & Boon author!

In the past, those of you who asked us for advice on how to write for Mills & Boon have been supplied with brief printed guidelines. Our new tape expands on these and, by carefully chosen examples, shows you how to make your story come alive. And we think you'll enjoy listening to it.

You can still get the printed guidelines by writing to our Editorial Department. But, if you would like to have the tape, please send a cheque or postal order for £4.95 (which includes VAT and postage) to:

VAT REG. No. 232 4334 96

AND THEN HE KISSED HER...

To: Mills & Boon Reader Service, FREEPOST, P.O. Box 236, Croydon, Surrey CR9 9EL.

Please send me _____ copies of the audio tape. I enclose a cheque/postal order*, crossed and made payable to Mills & Boon Reader Service, for the sum of £ _____ . *Please delete whichever is not applicable.

Signature _____

Name (BLOCK LETTERS) _____

Address _____

_____ Post Code _____

YOU MAY BE MAILED WITH OTHER OFFERS AS A RESULT OF THIS APPLICATION   ED1

Experience the thrill of 4 Mills & Boon Romances

An irresistible offer from Mills & Boon

Here's a personal invitation from Mills & Boon to become a regular reader of Romance. And to welcome you, we'd like you to have four books, an enchanting pair of glass oyster dishes and a special MYSTERY GIFT.

Then each month you could look forward to receiving 6 more brand – new Romances, delivered to your door, post and packing **free**. Plus our newsletter featuring author news, competitions and special offers.

This invitation comes with no strings attached. You can stop or suspend your subscription at any time, and still keep your **free** books and gifts.

It's so easy. Send no money now. Simply fill in the coupon below at once and post it to -

Reader Service, FREEPOST, P.O Box 236, Croydon, Surrey. CR9 9EL

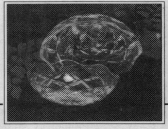

✂ - - - - - - - - *No stamp required* - - - - - - - - -

YES! Please rush me my 4 Free Romances and 2 FREE gifts!

Please also reserve me a Reader Service Subscription. If I decide to subscribe, I can look forward to receiving 6 brand new Romances each month, for just £8.10 delivered direct to my door. Post and packing is **free**. If I choose not to subscribe I shall write to you within 10 days - I can keep the books and gifts whatever I decide. I can cancel or suspend my subscription at any time. I am over18.

EP61R

NAME ⎯⎯⎯⎯⎯⎯⎯⎯⎯⎯⎯⎯⎯⎯⎯⎯⎯⎯⎯⎯⎯⎯⎯⎯⎯⎯⎯

ADDRESS ⎯⎯⎯⎯⎯⎯⎯⎯⎯⎯⎯⎯⎯⎯⎯⎯⎯⎯⎯⎯⎯⎯⎯⎯

⎯⎯⎯⎯⎯⎯⎯⎯⎯⎯⎯⎯⎯⎯⎯⎯⎯⎯⎯⎯⎯⎯⎯⎯⎯⎯⎯⎯⎯

⎯⎯⎯⎯⎯⎯⎯⎯⎯⎯⎯⎯⎯⎯⎯ *POSTCODE* ⎯⎯⎯⎯⎯⎯⎯⎯

SIGNATURE ⎯⎯⎯⎯⎯⎯⎯⎯⎯⎯⎯⎯⎯⎯⎯⎯⎯⎯⎯⎯⎯⎯

The right is reserved to refuse an application and change the terms of this offer. You may be mailed with other offers as a result of this application. Offer expires Dec 31st 1989 and is limited to one per household. offer applies in the UK and Eire only. Overseas send for details

mps MAILING PREFERENCE SERVICE